Also by Matt Haig

A Boy Called Christmas
Echo Boy
To Be A Cat
The Runaway Troll
Shadow Forest

The Girl Who Saved CHRISTMAS

MATT HAIG

with illustrations by CHRIS MOULD

CANONGATE

Edinburgh · London

For Pearl, Lucas and Andrea.
The most magical human beings I know.

Published in Great Britain in 2016 by Canongate Books Ltd,
14 High Street, Edinburgh EH1 1TE

www.canongate.co.uk

5

British Library Cataloguing-in-Publication Data
A catalogue record for this book is available on
request from the British Library

ISBN 978 1 78211 857 2

Typeset in 13.25/15pt Bembo by
Palimpsest Book Production Ltd, Falkirk, Stirlingshire

Printed and bound in Great Britain by Clays Ltd, St Ives plc

The Girl Who Saved Christmas

Do you know how magic works? The kind of magic that gets reindeer to fly in the sky? The kind that helps Father Christmas travel around the world in a single night? The kind that can stop time and make dreams come true?

Hope.

That's how.

Without hope, there would be no magic.

It isn't Father Christmas or Blitzen or any of the other reindeer that make magic happen on the night before Christmas.

It's every child who wants and wishes for it to happen. If no one wished for magic to happen there would be no magic. And because we know Father Christmas comes every year we know now that magic – at least some kind of magic – is real.

But this wasn't always the case. There was once a time before stockings and Christmas mornings spent excitedly ripping off wrapping paper. It was quite a miserable time, when very few human children had any reason to believe in magic at all.

And so, the very first night that Father Christmas ever decided to give human children a reason to be happy and to believe in magic, he had a lot of work to do.

The toys were in his sack, the sleigh and reindeer were ready, but as he flew out of Elfhelm he knew there wasn't enough magic in the air. He travelled through the Northern Lights but they were hardly glowing at all. And the reason for the low magic levels was that there wasn't much hoping going on. After all, how does a child hope for magic to happen if they have never seen it?

So that very first visit from Father Christmas nearly didn't happen. And that it did happen is thanks to one thing. A single human child. A girl, in London, who believed in magic totally. Who hoped and hoped for a miracle every single day. She was the child who believed in Father Christmas before anyone else. And she was the one who helped Father Christmas, just as his reindeer were starting to struggle, because the amount she hoped while lying in bed that Christmas Eve, added light to the sky.

It gave Father Christmas purpose. A direction. And he followed a thin trace of light all the way to her home at 99 Haberdashery Road, London.

And once that was done, once he had placed a full stocking of toys at the foot of her bug-ridden bed, the hope grew. Magic was there, in the world, and it spread among the dreams of all children. But Father Christmas couldn't fool himself. Without that one child, that eight-year-old girl called Amelia Wishart, hoping so hard for magic to be real, Christmas would never have happened. Yes, it took elves and the reindeer and the workshop and all of that, but she was the one who saved it.

She was the first child.

The girl who saved Christmas.

And Father Christmas would never forget it . . .

One year later . . .

Dear Father Christmas

Hello, my name is Amelia Wishart.
I am nine years old and I live at
99 Haberdashery Road in London.
      You know this because you have
been here. Last year. When you gave
me presents. That was very kind.
      I always believed that magical things
were possible, even when times were hard,
so it was so wonderful to see it was true.
      * THANK YOU *
Anyway, I live with my mum Jane
and my cat Captain Soot. I found
Captain Soot up a chimney. You see,
chimneys are rarely straight up and
down. Sometimes they have sideways
bits. Did you meet him? He is great.
      But he sometimes steals sardines
from the fishmonger and gets into
fights with street cats and I
think he thinks he's a dog.

I know you are a busy man so I will just tell you what I would like for Christmas. I would like: ❄ ❄

1. A new brush for sweeping chimneys.
2. A spinning top.
3. A book by Charles Dickens (my favourite author).
4. For my ma to get better.

Number 4 is quite important. It's more important than number 2. You can keep the spinning top.

It really was a magical thing to wake up to those presents last year.

Ma was a chimney sweep and now I am too. She can't go up chimneys anymore. She can't do anything anymore except lie in bed and cough. The doctor says only a miracle will fix her. But miracles need magic, don't they? And you are the only person I know who can do magic. So that is all I want.

I want you to make ma well again, before it is too late.

That is the main thing I ask. ❄

Yours faithfully,
Amelia

The Trembling Ground

ather Christmas folded up Amelia's letter and put it in his pocket.

He walked through the snow-covered Reindeer Field and past the frozen lake, looking around at all the quiet sights of Elfhelm. The wooden village hall. The clog shop and the Bank of Chocolate and the Figgy Pudding café on the Main Path, not open for another hour. The School of Sleighcraft and the University of Advanced Toymaking. The tall (by elf standards) offices of the *Daily Snow* on Vodol Street. Its walls of reinforced gingerbread, shining orange in the clear morning light.

Then, as he trod through the snow, turning west towards the Toy Workshop and the wooded pixie hills beyond, he saw an elf in a brown tunic and brown clogs walking towards him. The elf wore glasses and was a bit short-sighted so didn't see Father Christmas.

'Hello, Humdrum!' said Father Christmas.

The elf jumped in shock.

'Oh, h–hello, Father Christmas. I'm sorry. I didn't see you there. I've just been on a nightshift.'

Humdrum was one of the hardest working elves at the Toy Workshop. He was quite a strange, nervous little elf, but Father Christmas liked him a lot. As the Assistant Deputy Chief Maker of Toys That Spin or Bounce, he was a very busy member of the workshop, and never complained about working overnight.

'Everything all right at the workshop?' asked Father Christmas.

'Oh yes. All the toys that spin are spinning and all the toys that bounce are bouncing. There was a little bit of a problem with some of the tennis balls but we've fixed it now. They are bouncier than ever. The human children will love them.'

'Jolly good,' said Father Christmas. 'Well, you go home and get some sleep. And wish Noosh and Little Mim a "Merry Christmas" from me.'

'I will, Father Christmas. They will be very pleased. Especially Mim. His favourite new thing is a jigsaw with your face on it. Jiggle the jigsaw-maker made it especially for him.'

Father Christmas blushed. 'Ho ho . . . Merry Christmas, Humdrum!'

'Merry Christmas, Father Christmas!'

And just as they said goodbye they both felt something. A faint wobbling in their legs, as if the earth was shaking a little bit. Humdrum thought it was just because he was so tired. Father Christmas thought it was because he was so excited about the big day and night he had ahead of him. So neither said anything.

The Toy Workshop

The Toy Workshop was the largest building in Elfhelm, bigger even than the Village Hall and the *Daily Snow* offices. It had a vast tower and a main hall, all covered in snow.

Father Christmas stepped inside and saw the preparations were in full swing.

He saw happy, laughing, singing elves doing final toy tests: taking off dolls' heads; testing spinning tops; rocking on rocking horses; speed-reading books; plucking satsumas from satsuma trees; cuddling cuddly toys; bouncing balls . . . Music was provided by Elfhelm's favourite band, the Sleigh Belles, who were singing one of their favourites, 'It's Very Nearly Christmas (I'm So Excited I Have Wet My Tunic)'.

Father Christmas placed his sack down on the floor at the front of the room.

'Good morning, Father Christmas,' shouted one elf, called Dimple, with a cheery smile. Dimple's name was easy to remember because she had dimples in her cheeks whenever she smiled, which was always. She was sitting next to Bella, the joke writer, who was working on her last joke of the year and chuckling to herself as she ate a mince pie.

Dimple offered Father Christmas a peppermint and when he opened the lid of the peppermint jar a toy snake popped out. 'Aaagh!' said Father Christmas.

Dimple was now on the floor in hysterics.

'Ho ho ho,' said Father Christmas, and tried to mean it. 'How many of them do we have?'

'Seventy-eight thousand six hundred and forty-seven.'

'Very good.'

And then the Sleigh Belles saw him across the room and instantly changed their song to 'Hero In The Red Coat', which was a tribute to Father Christmas. It wasn't the Sleigh Belles' best song, but all the elves started singing.

'There's a man who's dressed in red,
With gifts for those asleep in bed.
A tall man with a snow-white beard,
Whose ears are round and rather weird.

He showed us elves that there's a way,
To make life as happy as Christmas Day.
He and his reindeer travel the world,
Giving presents to every boy and girl.
As all their hopes and dreams take float,
We all like to thank . . .
(Is it a goat?)
No!
It's THE HERO IN THE RED COAT!'

As the elves cheered, Father Christmas was a bit embarrassed and didn't know where to look, so he looked out of a window. He saw someone outside running across the snow towards the workhouse. No one else had noticed, as no one else was tall enough to see out of the window.

It wasn't an elf, Father Christmas knew that. It was even smaller. Too light. Too graceful. Too stylish. Too yellow. Too *fast*.

And then, realising exactly who it was, he left the workshop.

'Back in a moment, you wonderful folk,' he told the elves, as the music lulled. 'And the infinity sack is *there* so you can start dropping toys in it . . .'

By the time Father Christmas opened the door, she was there, hands on her little hips, bent double, breathless.

'Truth Pixie!' he said, happy to see her. After all, it wasn't often a pixie entered Elfhelm. 'Happy Christmas!'

The Truth Pixie's eyes, which were always huge, were even wider than they were normally.

'No,' she said, staring up at Father Christmas, from the height of his knees.

'What?'

'No. It's not a happy Christmas.'

The Truth Pixie stared inside the Toy Workshop and saw all the elves and felt a bit itchy, because she didn't like elves very much, and they gave her a bit of a rash.

'I've got a new suit,' said Father Christmas. 'It's even redder than it was before. And look at this fur trim. Do you like it?'

The Truth Pixie shook her head. She didn't mean to be rude, but she had to tell the truth. 'No. I don't like it at all. You look like a giant mouldy cloudberry. But that's not the point.'

'What is the point? You never come to Elfhelm.'

'That is because it is full of elves.'

Some of the elves had seen the Truth Pixie now.

'Merry Christmas, Truth Pixie!' they giggled.

'Idiots,' mumbled the Truth Pixie.

Father Christmas sighed. He stepped outside onto the snow and closed the door behind him. 'Listen, Truth Pixie, I would love to stay and chat, but it is Christmas Eve. I need to go and help get everything ready . . .'

The Truth Pixie was shaking her head.

'You need to forget about the Toy Workshop. You need to forget about Christmas. You need to get out of Elfhelm. You need to run for the hills.'

'What *are* you talking about, Truth Pixie?'

And it was then that he heard it. A kind of grumbling sound.

The Truth Pixie gulped.

'I knew I should have had a bigger breakfast,' Father Christmas said, patting his stomach.

'That wasn't coming from you,' said the Truth

Pixie. 'It was coming from down there.' She pointed to the ground.

Father Christmas stared down at the fresh snow, as blank as a white page.

'It's happening even sooner than I thought,' she squealed, and began running. She looked back over her shoulder. 'Find a safe place! And hide! And I suppose you should tell the elves to hide too . . . And you better cancel Christmas before they do . . .'

'They? Who are *they?*' But the Truth Pixie had gone. Father Christmas chuckled, looking at the pixie's tiny footprints in the snow heading back to the wooded hills. It was Christmas. The Truth Pixie had obviously been up all night drinking cinnamon syrup and was probably a bit confused.

Even so, he heard the rumbling noise again.

'Oh, stomach, do be . . .'

But the noise was much louder and lower and suddenly not that stomachy. It was a very strange sound. He was sure it was nothing to worry about. But even so, he went back inside and quickly shut the door so he could hear nothing but the sounds of the Toy Workshop.

Mr Creeper

eventeen days after Amelia Wishart had sent her letter to Father Christmas, she was where she very often was – inside a chimney.

It was dark inside chimneys. That was the first thing she had had to get used to. The darkness. Another thing was the *size*. Chimneys were always a bit too *small,* even if you were still a child. But the worst thing about being a chimney sweep was the soot. The black dust got everywhere once you started sweeping. In your hair, on your clothes, on your skin, in your eyes and mouth. It made you cough a horrid unstoppable cough, and made your eyes water. It was a horrible job but it was a job she needed. A job that could help her earn enough money for food and to get medicine for her mother.

And anyway, the thing about sweeping chimneys was that it made you enjoy daylight more. In fact, it made you enjoy being anywhere that wasn't a chimney. It made you hope. Being in the sooty darkness made you dream of all the exotic and light places in the world.

It was certainly no place to be on the morning of Christmas Eve. Stuck there, knees and elbows rammed against the chimney walls, choking on the clouds of soot as she brushed.

Then she heard something.

A tiny little crying sound.

Not a human sound. But something else.

A *miaow*.

'Oh no,' she said, knowing exactly who it was.

She pressed her heels against the chimney wall and felt around with her free hand in the dark until she reached something soft and warm and furry, lying on a sloping shelf inside the crooked chimney.

'Captain Soot! What have I told you? Never climb in chimneys! They are not for cats!'

Her cat began to purr as Amelia picked him up and carried him down towards the light of the living room. Captain Soot was black all over except for the white tip on the end of his tail. But today even that was as black as, well, soot.

The cat wriggled out of Amelia's arms, did a twisting jump through the air, and started to walk across the room. Across the cream-coloured rug. The *expensive* cream-coloured rug. Amelia stared at the sooty paw prints in horror.

'Oh no. Captain Soot! Come back! What are you doing?!'

Amelia went to get her cat but then of course *she* was getting the rug dirty too.

'Oh no,' she said. 'Oh no, oh no, oh no . . .'

She quickly got a wet cloth from the kitchen, where a knobbly handed kitchen maid was peeling carrots.

'I'm sorry,' Amelia said. 'I've just made a bit of a mess.'

The maid tutted and scowled, like a cross cat herself. 'Mr Creeper won't be happy when he gets back from the workhouse!' Amelia went back to the living room and tried to clear up the soot, but all she did was make the black marks look even bigger.

'We have to do this before Mr Creeper

comes back,' she told the cat. 'Of all the houses to choose to do this in, Captain!'

The cat said sorry with its eyes.

'It's all right, you weren't to know, but I bet Mr Creeper has got a temper.'

And as she kept scrubbing she realised there was something strange about this living room. It was Christmas Eve, and yet there wasn't one single decoration. Not one Christmas card. No holly and ivy. No smell of mince pies. Now, in a rich house like this one, this was quite unusual.

Then Amelia heard loud footsteps in the hallway. She turned as the living-room door opened, and there stood Mr Creeper.

Amelia stared up at the man. He was a long man. He had a long body. And a long, narrow face. And a long, crooked nose. And a long black cane that, with his dark coat and dark top hat, made him look like a crow who had decided – one dreary Tuesday while eating a worm – to become a human.

Mr Creeper was staring at Amelia, the cat and the smudged sooty footprints all over the floor.

'I'm sorry,' Amelia said. 'It's just my cat had followed me and he sneaked up the chimney.'

'Do you know how much that rug cost?'

'No, sir. But I'm cleaning it. Look, it's coming off.'

Captain Soot arched his back ready to pounce and hissed up at Mr Creeper. Captain Soot liked most people but he *really* didn't like this long man.

'Vile creature.'

'He's just trying to wish you Happy Christmas,' Amelia said, trying to smile.

'*Christmas,*' said Mr Creeper, and his mouth twisted as if the word had a horrid taste. 'Christmas is only happy if you are a fool. Or a child. And you are obviously both.'

Amelia knew who Mr Creeper was. He was

the man who ran Creeper's Workhouse, one of the largest workhouses in all of London. She also knew what a workhouse was. A workhouse was a horrible place. A workhouse was a place no one wanted to be but sometimes *ended up* if they became too poor or too ill or lost their home or their parents. It was a place where you had to work all day and eat disgusting food and hardly sleep and get punished all the time.

'What a pair of grubby little animals you are!' said Mr Creeper.

Captain Soot's hair stood on end, making him look like a fluffy ball of anger.

'He doesn't like being called names, sir.'

Mr Creeper clearly did not like being talked to in this way by a child. Especially a poor one, dressed in sooty rags, whose cat had made a mess of his floor. 'Stand up, girl.'

Amelia stood up.

'How old are you?'

'I'm ten, sir.'

Mr Creeper grabbed Amelia by the ear. 'You are a liar.'

He bent down and squinted at her as if inspecting some dirt on his shoe. Amelia saw his crooked nose and wondered how it had become broken. She silently wished she could have been there to see it happen. 'I spoke to your mother. You are nine. A liar and a thief.'

Her ear felt like it was going to be pulled off. 'Please, sir, that hurts, sir.'

'I could have gone for another sweep when your mother fell ill,' said Mr Creeper, letting go of Amelia and rubbing away the dirt from his hands. 'But no, I said I'll give this girl a go. What an absolute mistake. My workhouse is where you should be. Now, the money . . .'

'It's three pennies, sir. But as I made a bit of a mess you can have it half price.'

'No.'

'No what, sir?'

'You've got it the wrong way round. You are the one who has to pay me.'

'Why, sir?'

'For ruining my rug.'

Amelia looked at the rug. It probably cost more than a chimney sweep could earn in ten years. She felt sad and angry. She had needed the three pennies from Mr Creeper to buy a figgy pudding for her and her mother tomorrow. They couldn't afford a goose or a turkey but they could afford a Christmas pudding. Well, they would have done.

'What money have you got in your pocket?'

'None, sir.'

'Liar. I can see the shape of a coin. Give it to me.'

Amelia dug in her pocket to produce the only coin she had. She stared at the face of Queen Victoria on the brown halfpenny.

Mr Creeper shook his head. And looked at her, as if he really was a crow and she was a worm. He grasped her ear again and twisted it. 'Your mother really has been soft with you, hasn't she? I always thought she was a weak kind of woman. I mean, your father obviously thought so. He didn't stick around for either of you, did he?'

Amelia's face reddened. She had never known her father except as a charcoal sketch her mother had drawn. He was dressed in a soldier's uniform and was smiling. William Wishart looked like a hero and that was enough for her. He had been a soldier in the British Army and had gone to war in a very hot country called Burma. He had died there the year Amelia was born. She had imagined him being strong and noble and heroic and the exact opposite of Mr Creeper.

'Your mother has not been a good one,' continued Mr Creeper. 'Look at you. In your ragged trousers. You would hardly know you weren't a boy. Your mother hasn't taught you to be a girl, has she? At least she probably won't be around for long . . .'

Even Captain Soot seemed cross about this and he pounced across the room and swiped at Mr Creeper, digging his claws into his black trousers and ripping the material. Mr Creeper pushed the cat away with his cane, and Amelia felt a red flash of rage. She jabbed the sooty bristles of her brush into Mr Creeper's horrid face and kicked him in the shins. Then she kicked him again. And once more.

Mr Creeper coughed on soot. 'YOU!'

Amelia wasn't scared any more. She thought of her mother lying ill in bed. 'Don't. Talk. About. My. Ma!'

She threw the coin on the ground and stormed out of the room.

'I'll be seeing you.'

No, you won't, Amelia thought, and hoped like mad that it was true, as Captain Soot trotted by her side, leaving sooty footprints all the way.

Outside, Amelia walked eastwards, through the dark and dirty streets towards her home on Haberdashery Road. The houses got smaller and shabbier and closer together. A small church hummed with the sound of 'O Come All Ye Faithful'. As she walked she passed people setting up stalls for a Christmas market, girls in the street playing hopscotch, servants with geese from the butcher's, a woman carrying a Christmas pudding, and a man waking up on a bench.

A chestnut seller called out, 'Merry Christmas, love!'

Amelia smiled and tried to feel merry and Christmasy but it was hard. Far harder than it had been last year.

'It's Christmas Eve, love,' said the chestnut seller. 'Father Christmas will be coming tonight.'

Amelia smiled at the thought of Father Christmas. She raised her chimney brush and shouted, 'Happy Christmas!'

Little Mim

ittle Mim was an elf.

As you could guess from his name Little Mim was, well, *little*, even by elf standards. And young. He was younger than you. A lot younger. Three years old, to be exact. He had dark black hair that shone like lakes in moonlight and he smelled faintly of gingerbread. He went to the

little kindergarten that was now part of the School of Sleighcraft, and lived in a small cottage just off the Street of Seven Curves in the middle of Elfhelm.

But today wasn't a school day.

It was Christmas Eve. The most exciting day of the year. And this year it was the most exciting Christmas Eve there had ever been. At least for Little Mim. Because today he was going to see the Toy Workshop along with all the other elf children. You see, once Father Christmas's sack had been filled with all the presents for the human children, the elf children were allowed to pick whichever toys they wanted. And Little Mim had never been to the Toy Workshop.

'It's Christmas Eve!' he yelped as he jumped onto his parents' bed. His parents' bed, like most elf beds, was as bouncy as a trampoline, so the moment he jumped on it he bounced so high he hit his head on the ceiling and tore through a red and green paper chain that had been put up as part of the bedroom's many Christmas decorations.

'Little Mim, it's too early,' moaned his mother, Noosh, from beneath a tangled mess of dark hair. She pulled the pillow over her head.

'Your mummy's right,' said his father, Humdrum. He put on his glasses and nervously looked at his watch. 'It's a quarter past Very Early Indeed.'

Very Early Indeed was Humdrum's least favourite hour of the day, especially today, because he had been working all night. He felt like he had only just got into bed. Which he had. He loved being the Assistant Deputy Chief Maker of Toys That Spin or Bounce, which paid a reasonable one hundred and fifty chocolate coins a week and was a nice kind of job to have. But he also loved sleep. And now it was his son who was spinning and bouncing, such was his excitement.

'I love Christmas! It makes me feel sparkly!' Little Mim was saying.

'We all love Christmas, Little Mim. Just try and get back to sleep,' said Noosh, from under the pillow. The pillow was embroidered with the words 'It's Always Christmas In Your Dreams'. Noosh was tired as well, as this was an equally busy time of year for her too. She had been up late talking to reindeer.

'But, Mummy! Come on. It's nearly Christmas. We shouldn't do any sleeping near Christmas. So we can make it last longer . . . Come on. Let's build a snow elf.'

Noosh couldn't help but smile at her son.

'We build a snow elf *every* morning.'

Humdrum had fallen back asleep and was snoring. Noosh sighed because she knew this meant she wouldn't be able to fall back asleep now. So she took the pillow off her face and got up to make Little Mim breakfast.

'What were the reindeer saying?' asked Little Mim, as he ate his jam and gingerbread on a wooden stool in the small kitchen. He was staring at a portrait of Father Christmas that had been painted by local elf artist Mother Miro. It was one of seven portraits they had of him, and even though they knew Father Christmas was very embarrassed whenever he went to an elf's house and saw his own picture, they found it comforting having his strange bearded human face around.

'The reindeer didn't say much. They were very quiet. Comet seemed worried, which was unusual. And Blitzen was doing something strange.'

Mother Noosh was the *Daily Snow*'s Chief Reindeer Correspondent. Her job was to write articles about reindeer. The trouble was reindeer were really bad at interviews. The most you could get out of them was a grunt or a sigh. There was rarely a scandal unless you counted Blitzen doing a poo on Father Vodol's front lawn. (Father Vodol was Noosh's boss. And he had forbidden her from writing about that.) And a reindeer-related story never got near the front page, although there had been a little bit of interest in the fact that Cupid and Dancer kept falling in and out of love. And the annual School of Sleighcraft Reindeer and Sleigh Race had once made it to page four, but that was about it. Everyone knew that whichever elf had chosen Dasher would win, as he was the fastest reindeer by quite a way. It was officially the most boring job at the whole of the *Daily Snow* and Noosh wanted a more exciting role. Like Gingerbread Correspondent, or Toy Correspondent. But the thing she wanted to be more than anything was Troll Correspondent. She desperately wanted to be *Troll* Correspondent. It was the most dangerous of all jobs, because trolls were big and scary and had a long history of eating elves. But it was also the most important job, and by far the most exciting. And she wished every day that her boss would give her that job, but he never did. Father Vodol was a very grumpy boss. In fact he was the grumpiest elf in Elfhelm. And he hated Christmas.

'What do you mean?' wondered Little Mim, as his mother added ten spoonfuls of sugar to his cloudberry juice. 'Why was Blitzen acting strange?'

'He kept his head down. He kept looking at the ground. And he wasn't looking for food. He seemed quite worried. They all did. And last year they had all been excited. And anyway he looked at me and made a sound.'

Little Mim laughed because he found this funny. But Little Mim found everything funny.

'A bottom sound?'

'No. A mouth sound. It was like this . . .'

Noosh did the sound. She put her lips together and made a truffling kind of worried-reindeer sound. Little Mim stopped laughing at this because it was quite a troubling kind of noise.

Little Mim finished eating his gingerbread so, while his mother went to stand under the watering can in the bathroom, he played with a jigsaw. The jigsaw was another picture of Father Christmas. It had five thousand pieces and usually took Little Mim half an hour, which was quite slow for an elf. But then, just as he

 was working on piecing Father Christmas's red coat together, something happened. Parts of the jigsaw were disappearing, dropping into blackness. There was now a hole where Father Christmas's mouth should be. And the hole kept getting bigger as jigsaw pieces kept falling through the floor.

 'Mummy! The floor is eating Father Christmas!' shouted Little Mim.

But Noosh couldn't hear. She was in the shower, singing her favourite song by the Sleigh Belles. The song was called 'Reindeer Over The Mountain'.

Little Mim pushed his jigsaw aside and saw a dark crack in the tiles that was getting wider. Just then his mother appeared in her green day tunic, drying her hair with a towel that had a picture of Blitzen, Father Christmas's favourite reindeer, on it.

'What's that?' Little Mim asked her.

Noosh was confused. 'What are you talking about?'

'In the floor. It ate my jigsaw.'

Noosh looked. It was a crack. Right there in the shining green and white tiles near the wall. And not just any old crack. This crack was getting bigger and bigger until it stretched all the way across the small kitchen.

'What's that?' Little Mim asked again.

'What?'

'That sound.'

(Elves are very good at hearing, due to the clever curving of their ears, and child elves have slightly better hearing than fully grown elves. Which is why elf parents never talk nastily about their children.)

'It might be your papa snoring . . .'

But no. Now Noosh heard it. It too was a very deep low sound, coming from somewhere below. Noosh knew in an instant what the sound was, and her whole body froze in shock.

'Mummy?'

She looked at Little Mim and said one little word, 'Trolls.'

41

Humdrum Gets Out of Bed

T rolls.'

Even as Noosh said it she could hardly believe it. But she knew quite a lot about trolls. She had studied all there was to know. And she knew that although the Troll Valley was a long distance away, beyond the snowy wooded hills where the pixies lived, they mainly lived in caves that stretched deep under the ground. These caves stretched as far as Elfhelm.

'The peace is over . . . We've all got to get out of here.' She grabbed Little Mim's hand and pulled him away, just as more cracks appeared, making the kitchen floor look like a giant spider's web.

They ran into the family bedroom, which – as this was a small cottage with only one floor – was right next door.

'Humdrum!' shouted Noosh. 'Humdrum!'

She ran to the small sink in the corner of the room and picked up a bar of elf soap (just like ordinary soap, but smelling of berries).

'Papa, you've got to get out of bed! Trolls!'
Little Mim shouted as he shook his father.

Humdrum kept snoring for a second or so
until there was another roar from under the
ground. And Little Mim and Noosh watched
in horror as a crack started to appear in the
bedroom floor. The floor was opening up and
it was about to swallow the bed whole. The bed
was perched delicately over the large hole now.

'I had the most terrible dream,' mumbled
Humdrum, as he straightened his glasses. He
opened his eyes and saw – there in real life
– his wife and son screaming as a giant grey
warty troll hand rose out of the bedroom floor
to feel its way to the bed.

Noosh saw the vast size of the troll's hand
and knew instantly what kind of troll this was.
It was an übertroll. The second largest and third
stupidest of all seven troll species.

'Humdrum, get off the bed now. You've got
to run!' screamed Noosh.

But it was too late. Noosh saw the hand grab
her husband's leg and start to pull him into the
ground. Humdrum was not a particularly brave
elf. He was scared of lots of things. Shadows.
Loud music. The moon. Snowballs. So this was
too much for him.

Noosh ran and grabbed Humdrum's arm and tried to keep him in the room.

It was no good. Humdrum was inching further into the gap.

'Hold on, my little shortbread,' said Noosh, as she reached into her tunic pocket and pulled out the bar of soap. She rubbed it on the troll's warty skin. The skin smoked and burned and went red.

The troll roared in pain deep below and the hand flinched open. Humdrum fell to the floor, free again.

'Quick! Run!' Noosh cried and the three of them ran out of the room, Humdrum just in his underwear, as the ground continued to thunder and crumble beneath their feet.

When they made it outside, Noosh saw cracks in the street. The ground was shaking like an earthquake. Other elves were running out of their houses.

'Oh no!' Humdrum wailed as they saw their neighbour's house collapse. The wail got louder as their own house collapsed too. There was destruction and shaking all around them. Humdrum started to breathe really fast and turn a bit purple.

'Calm breaths, Humdrum,' said Noosh.

'Close your eyes and think of gingerbread. Like Doctor Drabble said.'

Whole houses were disappearing into the ground. Noosh spotted someone she knew from the *Daily Snow*. A big-eared bald-headed elf running out of the largest house on the street.

This was Father Bottom. The Troll Correspondent. He was meant to be the biggest troll expert in Elfhelm. He was now running with his hands in the air screaming, 'The trolls! The trolls! The trolls!' And pushing everyone out the way as he did so.

And even in her panic Noosh thought, *I really should have had his job.*

'Where shall we run to?' asked Humdrum, looking petrified.

There was only one answer Noosh could give.

'To Father Christmas!'

The Chamber Pot

So how did it go with Mr Creeper?' Amelia's mother asked from her bed between coughs as Amelia dealt with the chamber pot. The chamber pot was the round white tin pot they used to go to the toilet in. Amelia took the pot and opened the window and poured the yellow liquid out into the street.

'Oi! Watch out!' yelled a man below.

'Oops. Sorry,' said Amelia. Then she turned back to her mother and lied.

'It was all right at Mr Creeper's.' She didn't want to upset her mother with the truth.

'I'm glad you liked him,' her mother said, faintly, struggling for breath.

'I wouldn't go that far, Ma.'

'Did you get the figgy pudding?'

Amelia said nothing.

'I don't think I'll be able to eat tomorrow, anyway.'

Her mother was clearly struggling, but was

determined to speak. 'He has a workhouse . . . Mr Creeper.'

'Hmmm.'

'Listen, Amelia,' she whispered, 'I am not long for this world . . .'

Amelia could feel the tears in her eyes and tried to blink them away, so her mother couldn't see. 'Ma, don't talk like that.'

'It's the truth.'

'But, Ma.'

'Now, let me finish. When I die I want you to be looked after. I don't want you out on the streets. And even if you keep up your chimney sweeping you won't be able to stay 'ere, so I've spoken with Mr Creeper . . .'

Amelia felt her whole body go stiff with terror, and it had nothing to do with the bed bugs she could see crawling over the bed sheets.

'Stop this talk, Ma. You're going to get better.'

Her mother coughed again. The coughing lasted a long time. 'You'll be safe there.'

Amelia put the chamber pot back under her mother's bed. She stared at one of the bugs crawling on the sheets, going around in circles, before Captain Soot swiped it dead with his paw. She looked at her cat. He looked back at her. Captain Soot's glassy eyes were wide with shock at the conversation. Amelia doubted that cats were allowed in workhouses. And even if they were, she never wanted Captain Soot – or herself – to end up there. Especially as Captain Soot really seemed to dislike Mr Creeper.

'Come on, Ma, it's Christmas Day tomorrow. Magic will happen, you'll see. You've just got to believe . . . Christmas is when miracles can happen. Just wait, I promise . . .' And Amelia smiled and thought of the letter she had sent Father Christmas. She tried her very hardest to believe a miracle could happen and that – even in a world full of people like Mr Creeper – magic was always possible.

Her Mother's Hand (quite a short but very sad chapter)

It was an hour later. Amelia knelt and held her mother's hand. She was getting worse minute by minute. Amelia couldn't help but think of all the other – happier – times she had held her mother's hand. Walking along the river. Going to the fair.

Or when she had been little and her mother had held her hand after she'd had a bad dream. She remembered her mother's finger doing circles on her palm as she sang 'Ring a ring o' roses' in a soft voice to help her to sleep.

Her mother didn't speak much now because it seemed to take too much energy. But Amelia could see from her mother's frown that she had something to say.

Her mother shook her head. 'Amelia, my love, I'm afraid this is the end.'

She was breathing slowly. She looked as pale as milk.

'But you're not coughing.'

Her mother smiled the faintest of smiles. Amelia could tell it was a great effort for her mother to speak.

'Life will get better for you one day,' she told her daughter, as she had told her many times recently. 'Life is like a chimney – you sometimes have to get through the dark before you see the light.'

And her mother smiled a weak smile and closed her eyes and Amelia felt the hand she was holding grow heavy.

'Ma, you can't die. I won't let you. Dying is absolutely forbidden. Do you hear me?'

Jane Wishart closed her eyes. 'Be a good girl.'

And that was the last thing Amelia's mother ever said to her. There was no sound to be heard except the tick tock of the clock out on the landing and the sound of sadness weeping out of Amelia.

The Barometer of Hope

Father Christmas walked hurriedly through the workshop. Elves were swarming around him.

'Is that the infinity sack?' a short barrelly elf asked him, pointing to the sack he was holding.

'Yes it is, Rollo.'

'It doesn't look very big.'

'No, it isn't big. But it is *infinite*. You could fit a whole world in . . .'

And then the ground started to shake. Elves looked at each other with wider than usual eyes. Hobby horses clanked onto the ground. Toy carts slid back and forth across the stone floor. Rollo fell over hundreds of balls rolling across the floor and landed on his – fortunately large and cushiony – bottom. Then it went quiet and still again.

'What was that?' said Rollo.

'I'm scared,' said Dimple.

Bella started to cry.

Father Christmas turned to everyone.

'Just a little tremor, folks. Nothing to worry about. Even the ground gets excited near Christmas! Carry on as normal. We have a very big day – and night – ahead of us.'

And then Father Christmas swung the infinity sack over his shoulder and travelled up the chimney to the top floor of the workshop, to the Toy Workshop headquarters.

The moment Father Christmas stepped out of the chimney and into the Toy Workshop headquarters he saw the wise old elf Father Topo standing on the stone floor and stroking his long white moustache.

'All well, Father Topo?' said Father Christmas.

'Not exactly, Father Christmas. Didn't you feel the ground shake just then? I thought the whole tower was going to collapse.'

'Well, I felt a little tremor. But it will be fine. It must be all the magic in the air.'

'Hmmm. About that,' said Father Topo. 'Look at the Barometer of Hope. It should be bursting with light.'

He pointed at the Barometer of Hope, a small round glass jar positioned on a pole in the centre of the room.

The Barometer of Hope usually glowed with a dazzling display of multi-coloured, gently moving light. Green, purple, blue. These lights had been scooped up by Father Christmas from the Northern Lights in the sky above Finland. On Christmas Eve the light should almost be blinding, since it was fuelled by magic that grew out of hope and the goodness of elves, humans and all creatures.

But when Father Christmas looked up at the Barometer of Hope there was just a faint wisp of glowing green, flickering like a weak flame.

'Oh, I'm sure there's nothing to worry about,' Father Christmas said. 'It's glowing a little bit. It will pick up through the day. Come on, Father Topo. Cheer up! All the letters are still getting through!'

Just at that moment the normally smiling Mother Sparkle, from the letter room, ran into the headquarters, breathless. 'Something's going wrong! None of the letters are getting through to us. I've just heard from the letter catcher. They're not getting over the mountain.'

Father Christmas smiled. 'Oh well. The letters aren't getting through and there is a little glitch with the Barometer of Hope. It's not going to stop Chri . . .'

A distant but quite loud noise interrupted him. A roaring, crunching kind of noise. Father Christmas headed to the large window. In the distance he could see devastation on the Street of Seven Curves.

Whole houses were collapsing or disappearing into the ground. Elves were running along the cracking street in terror. Father Christmas gasped, and in no time at all Mother Sparkle and Father Topo were by his side.

Father Topo pulled his telescope from his top pocket. He saw a family running amid the chaos. And one of them was just in his underwear.

'Oh no. Noosh, Humdrum, Little Mim.'

Noosh was Father Topo's great-great-great-great-great granddaughter and the elf he loved most in the world.

It wasn't just the Street of Seven Curves that was under attack. The buildings of the Main Path were going under too. Workers from the Bank of Chocolate ran for their lives just before the bank was swallowed up into the ground.

Father Christmas could see something else. Where the Bank of Chocolate had once stood. He saw something crash through the heap of bricks and dust. First, a huge swathe of what looked like wild black hair was poking out of the ground. And then, slowly, a warty forehead. The kind of forehead that could only belong to a troll.

Father Christmas saw a rock flying through the air, coming from beyond the hills. It was heading – *wait, oh no* – it was heading straight for the Toy Workshop. It smashed through the window. Father Christmas pushed Mother Sparkle over and landed on top of her as the rock landed on the floor. Now, Father Christmas was a lot larger and heavier than an elf, so he squashed Mother Sparkle, but it was better, and softer, than being squashed by the rock. He got to his feet and went to the control desk and looked at the buttons and pressed the red one that said, in really little letters, 'VERY Serious Emergency!!!'

The bell above his head at the top of the tower started swinging at hyperspeed.

DINGDONGDINGDONGDINGDONG DINGDONGDINGDONGDING . . .

And it was then that Father Christmas

noticed the Barometer of Hope had smashed on the floor. The last green wisp of magical light rose towards him and disappeared into the air right in front of his face.

The Flying Story Pixie

So, this was Elfhelm on Christmas Eve. Shaking earth. Troll heads smashing up from below. Rocks and stones flying overhead. Buildings collapsing. Christmas puddings flying out of the Figgy Pudding café. Chocolate coins scattered on the ground. Elves carrying their children and running. The Sleigh Belles holding their instruments over their heads, to avoid the raining rocks.

'Elves!' boomed Father Christmas. 'Run to Reindeer Field! Everyone! Head to Reindeer Field!'

Father Topo was hugging Noosh and Little Mim, beside Father Christmas.

'Oh no,' said Humdrum, as the ground started to wobble beneath their feet again.

Noosh covered her son's eyes. Then the bulk of the Toy Workshop collapsed into the ground.

Father Christmas saw something rising out of the wreckage. One, then two, no, actually *three* trolls. These weren't big übertrolls. They were untertrolls, only three times the size of Father Christmas and nine times the size of an average elf. Well, technically there were four of them, because one of them had two heads. Another had only one eye. The third looked quite normal, for a troll, except for the one large yellow tooth sticking out from the side of her mouth. But each had warty rough skin and rotten teeth and dirty rags made from goatskin for clothes.

The one-eyed troll held a rock high in the air and let out a deep thunderous roar. He was looking at the remaining building in Elfhelm that wasn't yet destroyed. The five-storey office of the *Daily Snow*. He was about to throw the rock.

'Listen, trolls, we mean you no harm,' Father Christmas said.

The two-headed troll grabbed the one-eyed troll's arm.

'No, Thud,' the two-headed troll said. Thud shrugged and put his arm down.

'Thank you,' said Father Christmas. 'We just want a peaceful Christmas. We have no interest in the Troll Valley. Please . . .'

It was just at that point that Father Christmas heard something fluttering above. He looked up to see a creature a similar shape as the Truth Pixie, but this creature had wings and was much smaller. Four wings in total. Two sets of two. They were light, the wings, and you could see through them. They shone like glass, and the sun gleamed off them.

'A Flying Story Pixie!' said Noosh, who knew her pixies almost as well as she knew her trolls.

This pixie was circling around and giggling as she looked at all the mess the trolls had created. She flew down close to

Thud's head. Father Christmas saw this, and thought it was strange. Then the pixie disappeared, fast through the sky, heading into the trees on the snowy slopes of the pixie territory.

'Be no Christmas this year!' said Thud blankly. 'No Christmas!'

'What is your problem with Christmas?' wondered Father Christmas, perhaps a little unwisely, as Thud was still holding the rock. 'I thought trolls liked Christmas.'

Thud said nothing. Instead, he looked in the distance, somewhere towards all the elves in Reindeer Field. Then he made a massive grunting sound as he threw the rock high, high, high in the air. Everyone stared at the rock as it kept on going.

'Oh no,' said Father Topo, into Father Christmas's ear.

But Father Christmas could see where the rock was headed. Not to the elves, not to the reindeer, not to the *Daily Snow,* but towards the field where his sleigh was parked. The rock landed with a smash that could be heard a mile away.

Thud and the other trolls stamped their feet in a crazy fashion, as if doing a kind of wild troll dance.

'It's a signal,' Noosh said. She'd read about stomp signals in *The Complete Trollpedia* while training to be a journalist.

Below the earth there was another loud troll roar.

'Stand back, everyone,' Noosh warned, knowing what the sound was.

Then – *pow!* – a giant fist burst up through the ground. The grey fist alone was the size of one huge untertroll.

Humdrum was now crouched in a ball on the ground doing his breathing exercises while Little Mim said, 'It's all right, Daddy.'

'Urgula, the Supreme Troll Leader,' whispered Noosh. The fist disappeared back down into the ground, leaving nothing but a hole. Then the three above-ground trolls jumped, one after the other, down the hole. And the ground shook when they landed in the cave somewhere below.

Father Christmas looked around at all the

worried elves and the destroyed buildings and the collapsed Toy Workshop and waited for a few moments. Everything was still. The trolls had left them alone.

'They've gone,' he said.

And he heard Little Mim's faint mumble as he looked at the state of Elfhelm. '*Everything*'s gone.'

Father Christmas watched as a bouncy ball dropped out of the wreckage and rolled towards his feet.

Not quite everything.

A Knock at the Door

Down in London, a tall, well-dressed almost-skeleton stood at the door of 99 Haberdashery Road. Wearing a long dark coat and top hat, he was carrying a Bible and a shining black cane. His eyes were as grey as the creeping London fog on the street behind him.

Amelia tried to shut the door but Mr Creeper was too quick.

His face was really close. She saw him better than ever. His eyes had dark heavy bags below them. His damaged nose was as bent as a knee. His cheeks were so sucked in he looked as if he was entirely made of skin and bone. 'Never close the door on a gentleman. I am here to help you.'

Captain Soot was beside Amelia's ankles. He flicked his tail in a kind of warning.

'I don't like you,' the cat hissed. 'I know who you are and I don't like you one little bit. And I'm glad I ruined your rug.'

'I am sorry about your mother,' Mr Creeper said, not looking sorry or sad at all.

'How did you know?' Amelia said, looking down at his trousers. They were different to the ones Captain Soot had ripped earlier.

'Word travels to me.'

'Well, thank you, sir. Merry Christmas, sir.'

'So you aren't going to say sorry? For sticking your chimney brush in my face? For refusing my custom? For being a violent little brute?'

Amelia went to shut the door again but Mr Creeper grabbed her arm, tight.

'Go away and leave me alone, you smell-fungus!'

'You heard her,' miaowed Captain Soot.

Mr Creeper's smile had curled like a dead leaf under

his broken nose. 'No. Oh no. Unfortunately that is not possible. You are coming with me. You see, I have but one passion in this life. And that is the correction of mistakes. And your mother wants me to correct you. She told me that. You have too much of your father in you.'

Amelia knew her mother would never have spoken about her father in that way.

'It's my calling. At the workhouse we teach discipline. You are part of us now. It's time to take you away.' His nails dug into her arms.

No, it isn't, thought Amelia.

She looked down at Captain Soot, her eyes pleading for help. The cat looked at her intensely then trotted off into the living room.

Good plan, Captain Soot, thought Amelia.

Amelia yanked her arm free from Mr Creeper's tight grip and ran as fast as she could, into the tiny dark living room.

There were only two choices. The rotten old window or the small fireplace. Captain Soot was already at the fireplace.

'Good cat.'

There was no way Mr Creeper could manage the chimney.

'Get back here!' said Mr Creeper, his long,

crooked face glowering with hatred as he entered the room. 'You little mucksnipe!'

'Never!' spat Amelia as Captain Soot hissed the same thing. She scooped Captain Soot up off the floor. 'All right, Captain, let's go.' She crouched into the fireplace and disappeared into the darkness of the chimney.

Amelia placed her cat on her shoulder. 'Stay still, and no claws,' she said as she started to climb up the chimney using her elbows and pressing her feet against the sooty wall. It was extremely narrow, even by chimney standards, and the wall was crumbly and hard to stay steady against. She felt Mr Creeper's hand grab her foot. For a scrawny man he had a very tight grip. He started to pull her down, and she felt the rough pain as her elbows scraped the chimney wall. Heart thudding, she kicked him away, three hard kicks, and lost a boot in the struggle.

'Get back here, you demon child!'

But Amelia kept climbing up into the darkness. It was a tight squeeze, and got tighter as she neared the top. Captain Soot pushed his way through the chimney pot first. And Amelia then wriggled herself through. Amelia and Captain Soot had made it out into the light.

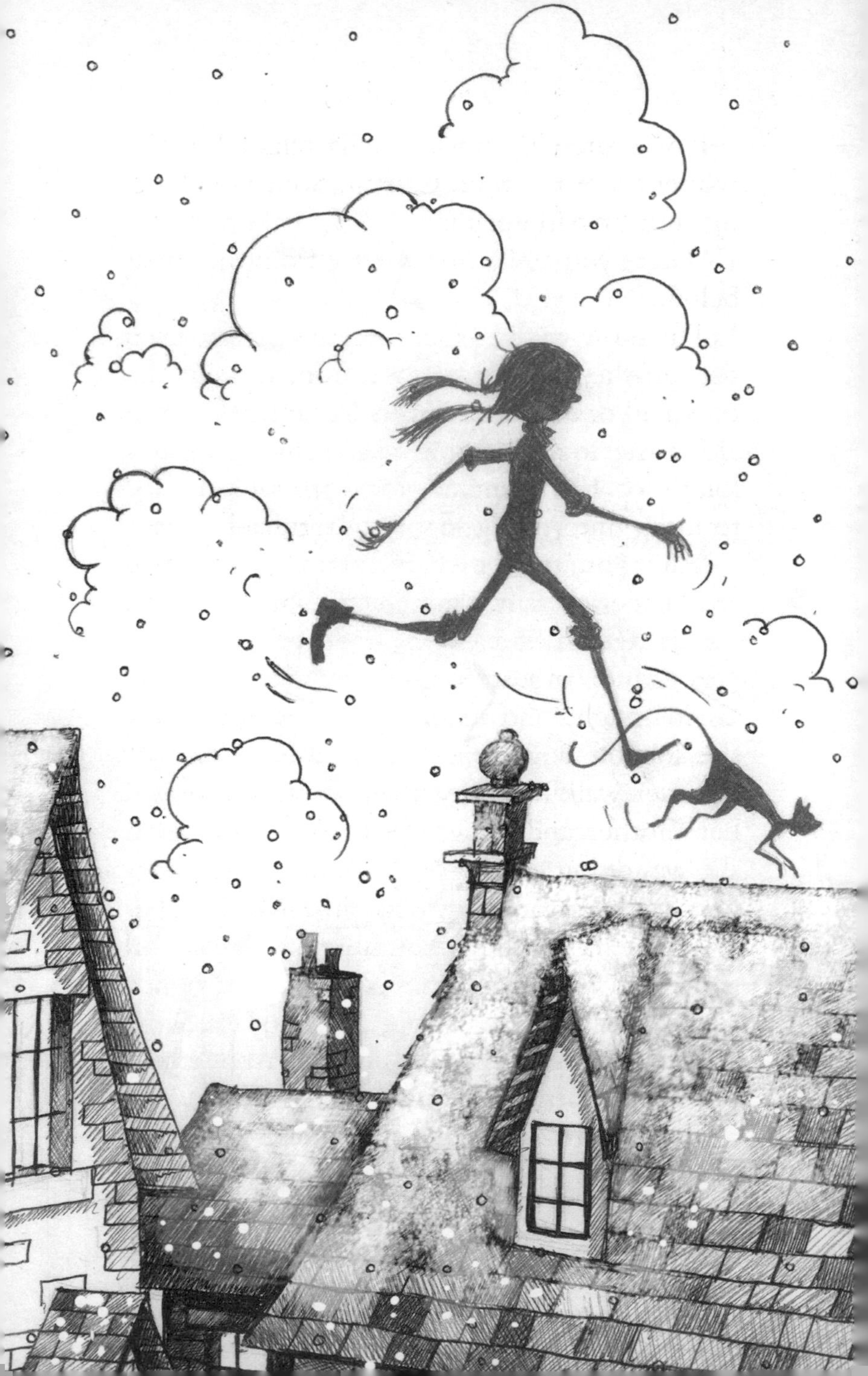

It was snowing now. Amelia blinked at the whiteness of the roof. Captain Soot ran along, making tiny footprints.

'There you are!' came a voice from the street below.

The snow was making the roof slippery. Even though she wasn't a cat and even though she only had one boot on, Amelia managed to run along the roof ridge without falling. It was a long roof. But eventually it ended and she had to jump onto the next row of terraced houses.

'After you,' said Amelia. Captain Soot jumped and made it, easily. Then Amelia jumped. And she made it. Less easily.

A group of carol singers stopped singing 'Silent Night' and stared up at her. Breathless, she looked down to the street and saw Mr Creeper walking fast with his cane. She loved her mother and knew she had thought what she was doing was for the best, but her mother hadn't understood how horrible Mr Creeper was. Amelia's mind was a storm of fear and panic and howling sadness.

'Aaagh!'

She lost her footing and slid down the other side of the sloping roof.

She caught hold of something. Hard and

wet and slippery. She didn't know what. But then she lost hold of it and she was falling and landing flat on her back. Looking around, she realised she was in somebody's backyard. Captain Soot ran after her and jumped and landed on her stomach.

'It's all right,' he told her, in the language of cats. 'You can do this.'

And Amelia understood him, for the first time in her life.

Amelia and Captain Soot got up and ran through the yard and into the passage behind the houses. They came out into India Street and heard the distant carol singers singing 'Good King Wenceslas'. Amelia looked behind and saw no sign of Mr Creeper. She ran fast, into the unknown land of her future.

Father Vodol and his Long Words

ather Christmas stood beside his broken sleigh as his oldest reindeer companion Blitzen came up and nuzzled him.

'It's all right, Blitzen.'

The elves were all standing in the snow eating emergency sugar plums for comfort, waiting for Father Christmas to say something.

So he did.

'Well.' He smiled. 'This has been a very unusual Christmas Eve. But it could be worse. Let's try and look on the bright side.'

'Bright side?' scowled an elf in a black tunic and long dark beard and thick bushy eyebrows. 'There is no bright side. It is a catastrophe. A calamity of epic proportions. A cataclysm. A ruination. A . . . a . . . poopleplex!'

Father Christmas sighed. Trust Father Vodol to try and bring everyone down further, while also showing off some very long words. Father Vodol was the elf who knew the most words. He knew all seventy-six million elf words, and sometimes even made some up, just to confuse people and sound really clever. Poopleplex wasn't a real word, Father Christmas was sure of it.

Noosh noticed Father Vodol's footprints in the snow. He had been walking from the west, from the hills, which was strange, as he was normally in the *Daily Snow* on Christmas Eve.

Father Christmas forced a smile. 'Come now, Father Vodol. There is always a bright side. Look, the trolls have gone. We are all safe. Obviously we will have to find out why this happened. And we will. We will. But that is not for today. Yes, there were some injuries, but we have incredible Elfcare workers seeing to those. Doctor Drabble is on hand. And we have the reindeer. Some buildings are still standing. Well, the *Daily Snow* is still standing. Elves can sleep there as we rebuild, or stay at my house. My bed can sleep about eleven elves, at least. And I could always sleep on the trampoline. But we must remember it is Christmas Eve, and we have work to do.'

A gasp spread across the crowd. Even Blitzen seemed doubtful, and did a wee to show just how doubtful he was.

'Christmas? Christmas!' scowled Father Vodol. 'You must be joking. There can't be a Christmas now.'

'Hooray!' said Little Mim, who didn't quite understand and just liked hearing the word. 'Christmas! Daddy, it's Christmas!'

Humdrum nodded and closed his eyes and tried to calm down by thinking of gingerbread.

Then Father Vodol stepped forward and muttered in a low voice, 'It's impossible.'

The crowd of elves gasped and parents put their hands over the ears of little ones.

'Father Vodol, please, no swearing. There are children present,' said Father Christmas, before continuing to address the crowd. 'I understand that it looks . . . difficult. But I was once told by a very wise elf that there is no such thing as im . . . that word. And every human child in the world is depending on us tonight. We have to give them magic.'

'I'm afraid Father Vodol might be right,' said Father Topo.

The elves seemed baffled.

'There are no toys!'

'There is no sleigh!'

Father Christmas nodded. 'Yes, there are concerns.' He looked at the smashed-up sleigh. 'The sleigh needs a bit of work. But we have the reindeer. And my good self. And the infinity sack. And there will be a whole world of hope. Every human child in the world will be filled with joy and excitement today. Later, when you look at the sky you will see the hope glowing in the air. The Northern Lights will be shining brighter than ever before.'

'Not to be a party pooper,' said Mother Breer, the beltmaker, 'but if that was the case then none of this would have happened in the first place.'

Father Christmas felt the paper in his pocket. The letter he'd got from Amelia Wishart. Amelia had been the first child he'd ever given presents to. He looked at Father Topo, who reached up and put his hand on Father Christmas's back. Or tried to. He could only really reach his bottom, which was a bit awkward.

'Come on, elves,' said Father Christmas. 'You are elves. We've at least got to try. The humans need us. Now, any questions?'

Little Mim put up his hand.

'Yes, Little Mim,' said Father Christmas. 'Fire away.'

'Can you spickle dance?' asked Little Mim. A few elves laughed. It was nice to think of spickle dancing on such an otherwise miserable day.

'Spickle dance? Erm, well . . .'

'I've never seen you spickle dance,' the little elf went on.

'Little Mim,' whispered Noosh. 'I don't think this is the time for such a question.'

'Little Mim, I am not an elf. Look at me. Look how tall I am. Look at my big belly. I mean, yes, I was drimwicked, but I still think spickle dancing is best left to elves.'

Little Mim looked sad. His smile faded. Even his pointy ears seemed to droop a little.

'Spickle dancing is for everyone,' chirped Little Mim. 'That is the *point* of spickle dancing.'

Father Christmas thought hard. If there was a chance of cheering the elves up, well, why not?

And then, to polite applause, he took a deep breath and started to move.

It turned out that Father Christmas was really quite a good spickle dancer.

'Right,' he said, out of breath, once he had finished. 'Shall we try and save Christmas?'

'I'll try!' came the same small voice from the front.

'Why, thank you, Little Mim.'

'Anyone else?'

Noosh raised her hand. And Father Topo. A few others did too. But Father Christmas had never seen the elves look so miserable.

'Right. Super. Wonderful.'

He patted Blitzen for comfort and looked over towards the mountain, thinking of the human world beyond, then hoped for the best.

Running

Amelia had run and run.

She ran west, without thinking, letting Captain Soot lead the way, through the dark of night. She followed his white-tipped tail like words chasing an exclamation mark.

After a while she realised it would be easier to run with no boots than with one boot and so she took her boot off and left it on the pavement.

She was crying as she ran, passing all the cosy houses with their curtains drawn and with happy Christmas Eve families sleeping inside. She thought of all the children who would wake up tomorrow and be happy with the toy soldiers or china dolls in their stockings. She had no idea what to do or where to go.

The old woman who sold roasted chestnuts was pushing her cart along the street. She had a kind face.

'Excuse me, Miss,' said Amelia.

''Ello again, gal,' she said, revealing a mouth

full of brown teeth. 'Shouldn't you and your cat be getting 'ome?'

Amelia felt desperate as cold and sadness bit into her. She hugged Captain Soot close. 'Erm, well, we have nowhere to go.'

The chestnut seller stopped pushing her cart and looked directly at Amelia.

'You ain't got no 'ome?' The chestnut seller sneezed. 'Oh no,' she said.

'No. Not one that is safe to go back to.' Amelia looked around. 'And Mr Creeper's after me.'

'You don't want that. A workhouse ain't no place for a young gal like you. Not his one, anyhow.' The woman sneezed again.

'Can me and my cat come home with you?' asked Amelia.

The woman looked at the ground.

'Ah'm afraid not, dear . . . Cats, I can't go near the things. Cats make me funny. That's why I've got the sneezes. Let me think . . . Let me think . . . Your best bet would be to 'ead to old Mrs Broadheart near Saint Paul's. She's a good soul. Tell 'er Bessie Smith sent ya. That's me. Bessie Smith. Mrs Broadheart looks after young girls like you . . . Selling matches might not be the best job but it's better to be a match girl than locked up in Creeper's Workhouse, I can tell ya.'

'Thank you,' said Amelia, walking away.

''Ere, have some chestnuts, love. Little Christmas present,' shouted the old woman.

But there was no time. Amelia saw a long shadow stretch from around the nearest corner. The shadow of a long thin man carrying a cane. She knew instantly who it was.

'I've got to go,' she said, and started running again.

'Well, good luck to you, gal.'

Officer Pry

Even though Amelia's bare feet were sore from running along the dark slush-puddled streets she kept running, dodging Christmas drunks and the warm sloppy contents of chamber pots. She reached Saint Paul's Cathedral, a massive building with a spectacular dome on top that looked like an onion dreaming of being much better and bigger than an onion. There were lots of people around, heading out of the church after the midnight service. But she couldn't see anyone who looked like she imagined old Mrs Broadheart would look.

She literally bumped into a policeman dressed in blue. When she was very little there hadn't been policemen about. Certainly not ones in smart uniforms. But now they seemed to be everywhere. This one had a very big fluffy moustache. It was as if the moustache had decided to grow a face rather than the other way around.

'Sorry, sir,' Amelia said.

''Ello, little girl,' he said. 'Now where you going?'

'I'm looking for Mrs Br . . .'

But before Amelia finished, a familiar voice interrupted.

'It's all right, Officer Pry. She's with me.'

Amelia turned and gasped as she saw Mr Creeper's face glowering under the gaslight.

Before she had time to run, one of his long bony hands had grabbed her arm.

'Oh, evening, Mr Creeper, sir,' Officer Pry said, taking off his hat.

Mr Creeper smiled his dead-leaf smile. 'Thing is, Amelia Wishart is a wild one. As wild as this horrid cat she's holding. She needs serious taming. New to us at the workhouse. I'd be ever so grateful if you helped me take her back where she belongs.'

'Yes,' said Officer Pry, grabbing her other arm. 'I see what you mean. She's a wild one. I'll help you back to the workhouse with her.'

'I don't belong there!'

But it was no good. Amelia was a girl with no shoes and no parents and no hope.

Charles Dickens

Mr Creeper looked at Captain Soot. Captain Soot hissed up at him. 'And you are going to have to get rid of that filthy animal too.'

Amelia's heart was racing with fear. Captain Soot was all she had. He was her best friend. However bad life got, Captain Soot had been there to lick her face or rub his head against her chin. And he was a cat who liked humans – except one.

A man was walking towards them. The man was slim and smartly dressed, wearing a bright purple coat, a top hat and smart winter gloves. He had a sharp but kind face and his eyes twinkled with intelligence. Amelia could see he was not only a rich man, with, most likely, a nice fireplace, but very probably the kind of man who would like a cat. Indeed, there was something a bit cattish about him.

The man stared straight at Officer Pry. 'What

is the occurrence here?' he asked, in a voice as rich as Christmas pudding.

'This child is a wild one. She belongs at the workhouse with Mr Creeper,' said Officer Pry.

The man then looked sharply at Mr Creeper himself. 'No child belongs at the workhouse, especially not at Christmas.'

'Bah,' said Mr Creeper. 'Humbug.'

'May I ask who you are?' enquired Officer Pry, looking the man up and down.

'I'm Charles Dickens. The writer. You've heard of me, surely?'

Charles Dickens! If this had been another day Amelia would have been very excited. Charles Dickens was her favourite writer. Father Christmas had given her his story *Oliver Twist* and she had loved it.

Mr Creeper shrugged and sneered both at once. 'Never heard of you.'

Charles Dickens crouched down so that he was head-height

with Amelia. He had a little dark beard starting to grow on the point of his chin. 'Where are your parents, dear girl?'

'Dead,' said Amelia. And a tear rolled down her cheek. Charles Dickens wiped the tear away.

Amelia felt embarrassed. 'Sorry, Mr Dickens.'

Charles Dickens smiled a worried smile. 'We need never be ashamed of our tears.'

Then Mr Creeper made a tutting sound. And this tutting sound was followed by Officer Pry saying, 'Now if you would be a good man and get out of our way, Mr Dickens?'

Amelia was so terribly sad that she was struggling to speak. But she knew this was her very last chance to save Captain Soot. 'Please, sir. Do you like cats? You see, they don't allow them where I am going . . .'

Now, Charles Dickens *loved* cats. Indeed he had just that morning written the words 'What greater gift than the love of a cat' into his notebook, thinking that one day he would put that line in one of his novels. He had a cat called Bob at home. And he was sure Bob would like a friend. 'I do like cats, but it would feel wrong to take this one from you.'

Amelia had to speak fast as she was being

dragged further along the street. Charles Dickens was walking alongside them as she told him, 'Well, it would still be mine. You'd just be looking after him. I'll pick him up when I escape.'

'You'll never escape,' muttered Mr Creeper as he pulled Amelia down a quieter street. This one was winding and dark. Right at the end of it was a tall and scary-looking stone building. It was grey – the grey of gravestones – and the street flickered in the ghostly light from the gas lamp. Amelia had a hunch this was the workhouse.

Officer Pry's moustache twitched. 'Sir,' he told the writer, 'if you don't leave us be, I will have to arrest you for being a public nuisance.'

Charles Dickens looked at the poor trembling cat and the poor trembling girl who held it. As Amelia neared the workhouse she put Captain Soot onto the ground.

'Go on, go to Mr Dickens,' said Amelia.

Mr Creeper stamped his foot to shoo the cat away. Captain Soot just stared at Mr Creeper's shoe, not the slightest bit scared.

'Go on,' Amelia said. 'Mr Dickens will look after you.'

And so Charles Dickens picked the creature up.

'I will indeed look after you.' It felt horrid to take the cat from her, especially at Christmas, but that is what he did, simply because he knew it was better for a cat to have a home than to live on the streets. 'And when you get out of the workhouse you can come and get him. He'll be with me. At 48 Doughty Street. In Bloomsbury.'

'He likes fish!' said Amelia desperately, as she was pulled closer towards the workhouse.

'Then he shall have the best sardines every single day.'

'And his name is Soot. And he is a captain.'

Charles Dickens nodded. 'Oh yes. So he is. Captain Soot. Very well!'

The cat stared sadly after Amelia. 'I'll miss you,' he miaowed. And Amelia stared sadly after the cat. And Charles Dickens stayed standing in the street, watching the raggedy, soot-covered, bare-footed orphan girl head off to spend Christmas in the workhouse. Then he carried the cat home, walking past a man coming out of the pub next door.

'Happy Christmas!' the man said.

'Yes,' said Charles Dickens, who couldn't bring himself to say 'Happy Christmas' back.

'Isn't it the best of times?' the man went on.

The cat gave a gentle miaow of disagreement in his arms as Charles Dickens nodded. 'Yes. And the worst.'

The Dark Sky

They didn't find much left from the Toy Workshop. Five spinning tops, seven bouncing balls, ten packs of playing cards, twenty-one dolls and a squashed satsuma.

The sky was dark but Father Christmas kept singing to try and keep everyone else's spirits up.

'Jingle bells, jingle bells, jingle all the way, Oh what . . .'

But only Little Mim was joining in.

Then Kip came over to speak to him. Kip was Elfhelm's sleigh expert, and ran the Sleigh Centre on the Main Path, which had been destroyed by the trolls.

Kip was a quiet elf. Narrow and tall, but with a bit of a stoop, he looked like a walking question mark. You had to be quite close to his face when he talked. He had been kidnapped as a child and Father Christmas had rescued him, and ever since then they had had a special friendship.

'Hello there, Kip,' Father Christmas said, holding a single dusty domino he had just found, as he climbed off the wreckage. 'Can you fix the sleigh?'

Kip shook his head. 'No. It's impossible.'

Father Christmas winced. 'Why is everyone swearing today?'

Then Kip told him *why* it was impossible. 'The compass is broken, the frame is smashed, the seat's disappeared, the reindeer harness is ripped to shreds, the hope converter and propulsion unit have combusted, the speedometer is down, the altitude gauge has bust, the undercarriage is completely beyond repair, the upholstery is destroyed, the launch and landing runners have fallen off, and the back-up manual steering function is out too. Oh, and the clock's gone.'

Father Christmas nodded. 'But other than that it's fine?'

'It won't even get into the air, let alone fly around the world.'

Father Christmas looked down at the blank dotless domino in his hand. 'All right, Kip. Thank you.'

A moment later Father Christmas was sitting in the snow, wondering what to do, when Father Topo came over to him carrying a cup of hot chocolate. He had a copy of the *Daily Snow* under his arm.

'Let me see that,' said Father Christmas.

Reluctantly the old elf held out the newspaper.

'TROLL TERROR STOPS CHRISTMAS.'

'Father Vodol really knows how to keep people's spirits up, doesn't he?'

Father Topo smiled. 'Misery sells newspapers. But listen, I'm afraid in this instance he is right, you need to forget about Christmas.'

'But what about all the children?'

'Well, most remember how it used to be. Before last year. It will be just like that again. And it's only for this year. We'll be back next year.'

'But what if we're not?' asked Father Christmas.

Father Topo had no answer. And he normally had an answer for everything.

The Falling Reindeer

Father Christmas headed over to his reindeer, carefully treading over the cracks in the earth.

He could see the reindeer were still in a state of shock.

'It's all right, my deers. I know we have had a nasty surprise, but we must do what we can to try and carry on as normal. Are you with me?'

None of the reindeer could look him in the eye. Blitzen chewed some snow. Dancer and Cupid were nuzzling each other. Vixen bit Comet's ear for sniffing her bottom. Dasher was nervously walking around in circles. And Prancer was pretending to be interested in her own hooves.

'Now, we have no sleigh and nowhere near enough presents, but I'd like to try and cheer up as many human children as possible. I will just need one of you. Just to ride on your back. It is going to be a tough night, so I need someone who believes we can do this.'

The reindeer all looked at each other, then

at Father Christmas. Prancer's eyes said, 'You must be joking.'

But then, to Father Christmas's joy, Blitzen stepped forward.

'You're a true friend, Blitzen,' he whispered in his ear as he tried to climb on the reindeer. He hadn't ridden on a reindeer's back for years, so he had lost the knack and fell head-first in the snow on the other side. Comet did a little reindeer giggle. But Father Christmas was second time lucky.

'There. Easy,' he said.

He looked at the sky and searched for signs of the Northern Lights. He needed to get high enough into the sky to cover himself with the Northern Lights – with all those particles of magic and hope that filled the air at Christmas. Then magic would happen. Time would stop. It was Christmas night so the sky should have been filled with green and blue and pink light, but there was nothing. Nothing but darkness and the moon and the stars. The sky was still just an ordinary sky.

He pulled out his pocket watch. It was ticking forward. It was ten minutes to Almost Bedtime.

There is no impossible . . .

'Come on, Blitzen, we can do this. Let's go find the Northern Lights.'

Blitzen began to gallop. He galloped and galloped and galloped. He was the strongest and second fastest (after Dasher) of all the reindeer and they were going very fast across the ground, jumping over the large cracks and debris that the trolls had caused.

Then Father Christmas leant forward and held onto the antlers.

'Right, Blitzen, fly. Fly *now*. You can do it. Fly, fly, fly!'

Blitzen was trying, there was no doubt about that. But trying and flying are two different things. Even Father Christmas became worried as they approached the frozen lake at the edge of Reindeer Field.

'Come on, Blitzen!'

And Blitzen did it. The sound of hooves over snow became the sound of silence as the hooves began to tread on air, galloping higher into the sky.

'Yes, Blitzen! We did it!'

Father Christmas looked down

to his right, to the south, and saw the rubble that was now Elfhelm.

It was as if an angry child had built up a toy village and smashed it in a tantrum. Father Christmas noticed the *Daily Snow*, the one building still fully standing. *Must have been all those expensive building materials Father Vodol used*, thought Father Christmas. *All that reinforced gingerbread.*

Then he felt Blitzen start to dip.

'Blitzen? What's wrong? We're meant to be getting higher!'

But they were dropping quite fast, out of the sky. They crash-landed on Silver Lake, where Blitzen – not being much of an ice-skater – skidded along wildly, his hooves going in every direction as he spun around in circles.

Father Christmas got quite dizzy until they bumped into the bank at the side of the lake, which sent him flying through the air, doing a little round somersault before landing on his back with a heavy thud onto the snow. Father Christmas just lay there a short while, staring up at the sky, trying his hardest to see a magic that wasn't there, and feeling that letter from Amelia in his pocket that he would never be able to answer.

The Soap

The workhouse was a very large sinister-looking place made of dark stone, that stood on its own on one side of the street, as if other buildings were too scared to go near it. There was a large black metal gate and a grim murky green front door. It sat under dark clouds and looked like a huge prison.

'Thank you, Officer Pry, I can take it from here,' Mr Creeper said. He handed Officer Pry some money.

'Oh, thank you, sir. Thank you.'

Officer Pry looked at Amelia. 'Now do as good Mr Creeper tells you.'

'I don't belong here!' Amelia shouted at the policeman as the gate closed like hope behind her.

Mr Creeper dragged her into the workhouse.

'No one belongs here,' he said, scratching his broken nose. 'That's the whole point.'

A woman was there to greet them. Dressed in a navy starched cotton dress, she was short

and thin and had a large chin. She looked as though she was sucking a lemon. Her nose sniffed at Amelia with disgust.

'The new arrival, Mrs Sharpe.'

'What is this filthy thing?'

'Speak!' Mr Creeper said, jabbing Amelia with his cane.

'My name is Amelia.'

'Amelia?' asked Mrs Sharpe. 'It sounds like "ameliorate". That means "to make something better", which must be quite easy when you start off with something like you.'

Then she laughed a low little laugh that followed Amelia inside like a ghost of lost happiness.

However bad the workhouse looked from the outside, nothing could compare to what it was like inside. It was a place of sharp angles and hard edges. A place of corridors and dormitories and workrooms. The walls were all painted in a kind of dark brown, which was the gloomiest colour Amelia had ever seen and made her heart feel heavy just by looking at it. A weak old man with a sad face was painting over the wall with exactly the same paint. Amelia looked at the paint tin and saw the label: 'Gloomy Brown Paint'.

There was absolutely nothing about the place that suggested it was Christmas Eve.

'The work never ends here,' Mr Creeper said, enjoying the idea. 'I will leave her with you, Mrs Sharpe.' Then he turned to Amelia. 'I must go home. I have the chimney sweep coming. He's *so much* better than the last one I had. Vulgar little creature she was.'

And then he was gone and Amelia was left with Mrs Sharpe.

'Right then,' Mrs Sharpe said. 'Bath time.'

They arrived at a wooden door with paint peeling off it like scabs. Mrs Sharpe opened it to reveal a large cold room with a bath in the middle of it and an atlas of damp patches on the walls.

Mrs Sharpe made sure Amelia had the coldest bath of her life, which even her tears couldn't warm. Then Mrs Sharpe handed her something that looked like a sack.

'What's that?' asked Amelia.

Mrs Sharpe shook her head. 'There are no questions in the workhouse.'

But by now Amelia had worked out that the bundle in her hands wasn't a sack. It was clothes.

She put on the horrid baggy uniform. 'It's itchy.'

Mrs Sharpe nodded, as she roughly used a comb to untangle Amelia's hair.

'Stop that!' Amelia shouted. 'Get off me, you . . .' Amelia wasn't really thinking. She was tired and weak and sad and having the worst day of her life and the next word just came out of her as her hair was being yanked. '. . . monster.'

Mrs Sharpe was furious. She picked the bar of soap out of the bathwater and said, 'Open your mouth!'

'No,' said Amelia.

'You wretched girl! Open your mouth or you'll be locked in the basement!' Amelia opened her mouth and nasty Mrs Sharpe rubbed the soap over Amelia's tongue. Amelia closed her eyes and felt sick at the horrid wet soapy taste forced into her mouth. But she was determined not to show it so she decided to comfort herself by calling Mrs Sharpe every rude name she could think of – in her head.

Monster!
Witch!
Flapdoodle!
Hornswoggler!
Foozler!
Gibface!

And then, once Mrs Sharpe had finished washing her mouth out she marched her down a long corridor and showed Amelia where she was to sleep. A grim dormitory with thirteen others. Her bed was hard wood with a very thin mattress.

'You get four hours' sleep a night. So make the most of it.'

'When can I leave?' Amelia asked.

Mrs Sharpe looked shocked at the question. 'Leave? *Leave*? You ain't leaving, Miss. You are here for a very long time indeed.'

The door closed. The girl in the bunk above her was snoring.

Will I still be here next Christmas? Amelia wondered. *How could anyone survive a year in this place? Or two years. Or three.*

She closed her eyes and thought of time. If only she could go back in time to be with her mother again. Or forward to when she could leave this place.

She was going to make a wish, but realised wishes were pointless now. Who would she wish to? Father Christmas? No. It was down to her.

'Next Christmas I won't be here,' she whispered, making a promise to herself.

And she tried her hardest to believe it.

One year later . . .

Noosh's New Job

It had taken a year for Elfhelm to be rebuilt but elves were hard workers and now the whole place looked better than ever.

The only building that hadn't needed any work doing, of course, was the office for the *Daily Snow*, which stood at the end of Vodol Street, just off the newly paved Main Path. There were now lots of other buildings around it. The shops and houses had been built with added trollproofing (bricks made of soap, trampoline suspension) and they all looked sparkling and new, especially the golden Bank of Chocolate, but still none was as impressive as the old *Daily Snow* building. It was made from the most expensive materials chocolate could buy (reinforced gingerbread, pixie wood, hardened marzipan, pure clear North Pole ice for the windows).

Noosh stood nervously in Father Vodol's impressive office, on the top floor. Father Vodol was no longer leader of the Elf Council. That

job, of course, belonged to Father Christmas. But Father Vodol was the richest elf in Elfhelm, and earned seven hundred chocolate coins a minute. He didn't even like the *taste* of chocolate. And so he was also the only elf in Elfhelm who didn't waste his money by eating it.

'Noosh,' said Father Vodol, sitting in a chair twice his size as Mother Miro, the most famous artist in Elfhelm, painted his portrait. The portrait was to be a Christmas present to himself, to go with the seventeen other portraits of himself lining the walls. 'Thank you for coming to see me.'

'That's all right.'

'Now tell me, Noosh, are you happy chatting to reindeer?'

Noosh thought. She wasn't really happy being Reindeer Correspondent, and Father Vodol knew this. 'Yes. It has its moments,' she said. 'Sometimes. I suppose. Not really. No. I hate it.' She looked nervously around, and noticed his chest of drawers, where he filed long words away.

'So if I said to you that I want you to become Troll Correspondent, what would you say?'

Noosh tried to think what to say. And then she said, 'Bottom!'

She went a bit red. 'I mean, what about Father Bottom?'

'Well, Father Bottom has been to see Doctor Drabble and he has trollophobia. He closes his eyes and he sees trolls. He can't go near them. He can't leave his house. He can't write about them now. It's quite a problem when you are the Troll Correspondent. Do you understand?'

Noosh understood.

'So, you know what day it is, don't you?'

Noosh nodded. 'Christmas Eve.'

Father Vodol looked a bit grumpy. He had a problem with Christmas, Noosh realised. 'That's not the important bit. This is the first anniversary of Troll Attack Day. That terrible calamity. And Father Bottom has had a year – a whole year! – and he still hasn't found out the truth. This is the biggest story there has been since the beginning of stories. It is huge. Gargantuan, monumental, colossal.' He smiled as he said this, because he loved saying long words. 'And it could be yours . . .'

Noosh didn't know what to say. But she noticed something

outside the window. Something hovering. A small, beautiful, little four winged boy-creature, wearing silver clothes. A Flying Story Pixie. She remembered all the other ones she had seen, starting with the day of the troll attack. They seemed to be everywhere these days, for some reason. The creature knocked on the glass.

The grumpy black-bearded elf noticed and he narrowed his eyes and shook his head at the creature. The pixie looked confused, but then flew sadly away.

'Odd creatures.'

'They have special powers,' Noosh said. 'They can hypnotise you just with their words.'

'Well, I wouldn't know anything about that,' Father Vodol said quickly. 'So, Noosh, what do you say?'

'I don't know,' she said. 'It's quite a lot to think about.'

Father Vodol smiled. 'It won't be dangerous. Even last year, they made sure no elves were actually killed. Take a few bars of soap if you want to be safe. You'll be fine.' Then he asked Mother Miro to turn the portrait around. It looked exactly like him.

'It looks nothing like me,' he said. 'Does it look anything like me, Noosh?'

'Erm . . .'

'Exactly. It looks nothing like me.' Then he flapped Mother Miro away and focused on trolls again.

'There have been noises,' he said.

This was news to Noosh. 'Have there?'

'Yes. Underground. Last night. And the night before. They could be building up to another attack. We need someone to find out what is going on. To go and interview the Supreme Troll Leader.'

Noosh felt her heart thump with dread. 'Urgula?'

'Yes. We have no reason to fear her. Yes, she is large. The largest creature in existence. But there have been *Daily Snow* interviews with her before.'

'Not for years.'

'Time doesn't change things that much. What do you think, Noosh? This is your big break.'

Noosh felt nervous. She thought of Little Mim and she thought of Humdrum. They pulled a cracker in her mind. 'But, but, it's Christmas.'

Father Vodol laughed. He hardly ever laughed but when he did it lasted a long time. Noosh looked at her watch. It was ten past Not So Early Any More.

'But my family will want me home for tomorrow . . .'

'You'll be back by morning. And if you get an exclusive on the trolls, you and your family will be rolling in chocolate coins for the rest of your life. This is what you always wanted, isn't it? And besides, you'll be helping save Elfhelm. The last thing we want is a repeat of last year . . .'

So Noosh went back to her home, which was in exactly the same place as her old home and looked exactly the same too, complete with the seven portraits of Father Christmas hanging on the wall. Little Mim was bouncing on the trampoline bed as usual. Humdrum was eating his sugar plums in a hurry as he was running a little late for the workshop on the most important day of the year. As always, he was fretting about pretty much everything there was to fret about.

'I can't be late . . . there's so much to do . . . so many balls to bounce and tops to spin . . . so much needs to be checked . . . And what if the trolls come back?'

Noosh went pale. She knew she should tell

her husband about her trip to the Troll Valley but how could she? Humdrum would die with shock. So she said nothing except a quick goodbye as he left the house.

Little Mim did a big bounce and jumped off the trampoline bed and landed in his mother's arms. 'It's nearly Christmas!' he said, and he kissed her ear.

She remembered Little Mim's excitement last year, just before the trolls attacked. She knew that this must never happen again. 'Yes, it's Christmas Eve. So that means this afternoon you and all the other elf children can go to the Toy Workshop and choose some toys.'

'Hooray!' said Little Mim.

'But first you need to get ready. You're going to the Christmas party at the School of Sleighcraft. All the kindergarten is invited. The Sleigh Belles are even playing . . .'

Little Mim, like his mother, loved the Sleigh Belles. They were his favourite band and their number one hit 'Reindeer Fly Over The Mountain' was his absolute favourite song. But Noosh wondered why a frown had appeared on his little face.

'The trolls aren't coming, are they?'

'No, they're not coming,' Noosh said. But

then she thought. And then she looked at her son's wide, wide eyes and knew she couldn't lie to him. 'I have been asked to go to the Troll Valley, Little Mim. For an article.'

Little Mim's eyes widened. 'You're going on a scary adventure!'

'Not really. It's just a little day trip. A little adventure. I need to find some information. It's just beyond the wooded hills. I will be back very soon, I promise. But for now this is our secret, okay? All right, my little cloudberry?'

She held her son close and smelled his clean sweet hair. She couldn't have loved anyone more. 'It's going to be fine,' she said. 'It's just something Mummy has been wanting to do.'

And Little Mim stared up at his mummy and thought he would like a little adventure too, but maybe not one involving those horrible trolls that had destroyed last Christmas, and who had caused his father to have so many nightmares.

He didn't like the idea of his mum going all on her own to the Troll Valley. So he decided to make a plan of his own, and keep it as his little secret.

The Truth Pixie

Noosh held Little Mim's hand as they walked through the snow to the kindergarten. The whole of Elfhelm was busy with excitement.

Elves were walking past with bundles of new elf-made clothes or holding as many chocolate coins as they could carry. They were all heading to Reindeer Field, where Father Christmas would be opening up his infinity sack for them to drop in the gifts for human children. Noosh felt sad that she was missing Christmas Eve, but if – as Father Vodol thought – the trolls really were planning another attack, then Elfhelm needed to know about it.

Noosh left Little Mim at the kindergarten gates, and after a small kiss on his forehead she hurried away, passing the gingerbread shop and thinking of Little Mim who loved biting the heads off gingerbread elves. It was then she had a horrible and scary thought.

The thought was: *what if I never see him again?*

Noosh left the Main Path and turned down Quiet Street and took a left down Really Quiet Street then turned right at the Secret Route to the Wooded Hills. She had been to the Wooded Hills many times in her life. When she was a little girl Father Topo had taken her pixie spotting. She had captured a Flying Story Pixie in a jam jar and been mesmerised by its wings. When Father Topo saw the poor trapped pixie he was very cross. He freed the pixie and gave it a new word. The word was 'miscellaneous' and the Flying Story Pixie liked it very much. Flying Story Pixies fed on words the way some creatures feed on honey and they were always on the hunt for new words, exotic words, with which to spice up their stories.

The snow was thicker here on the Wooded Hills than it was in Elfhelm and everything was uphill, so Noosh quickly became tired. Her feet trudged through the snow, and stumbled on pine cones. She felt a bit guilty that she hadn't told Humdrum but he would have been worried and told her not to go. Humdrum was all right, as husbands went, but he was a worrier. He worried about everything. Not just trolls. He worried about breaking his teeth on candy cane. He worried that the sun would forget to rise. He worried that one day all balls in the workshop would just stop bouncing and spinning tops would stop spinning. He worried, most of all, that the trolls would return. Still, she couldn't help that guilty feeling in her stomach, which was a bit like the feeling of falling. She saw, through the prickly pine trees, a tiny yellow cottage up ahead, with a small wooden door. It was a pixie cottage, less than half the size of an elf cottage.

The cottage was so bright, like the yellowest cheese, with a steep roof, as if it was an arrow pointing at the sky. It had one little window and one little door.

There was a little sign on the door.

'WARNING' it said, 'I TELL THE TRUTH.'

So this is where the Truth Pixie lives, Noosh thought. And she remembered that Father Christmas liked the Truth Pixie, so she shouldn't be too scary. Noosh knocked on the door.

A small, delicate creature with saucer-wide eyes and pointed ears and a bold dress sense (yellow, yellow, yellow) appeared. She smiled a big, mildly mischievous but very happy smile.

'You are the Truth Pixie,' said Noosh.

The Truth Pixie looked up at the elf. 'Yes, I am. Thanks for telling me. Bye.'

The Truth Pixie closed the door in Noosh's face.

Noosh stayed where she was and spoke loudly at the wooden door. 'Sorry. I just wanted to ask you some questions. I'm a friend of Father Christmas. I am trying to find out if there is going to be another troll attack. And I know you are a pixie, not a troll, but pixies tend to have more information than elves about such matters so I just wondered if you . . .'

The door opened. The Truth Pixie was there. Her huge eyes looking up at her.

'So, you're a friend of the big man?'

'Yes,' said Noosh, with the pride of someone who owned seven Father Christmas portraits.

'Enter,' said the Truth Pixie. 'But leave your clogs outside.'

So Noosh slipped off her clogs and left them in the snow by the door then went inside.

It was bright yellow on the inside too, and smelled of cinnamon. Noosh sat on a chair.

'I would offer you some cinnamon cake but I want it all for myself,' the Truth Pixie told her.

'That's all right,' said Noosh, over her

rumbling stomach, as she took out her notebook. 'Is it okay if I write some notes down for the article?'

'Yes. But don't quote me. I like my "air of mystery". I've been working on it for years.'

The Truth Pixie stared at Noosh. 'Elves are so strange-looking,' she said. 'With your thick fingers and wide faces and your legs like tree stumps. I mean, you don't look as strange as Father Christmas with his freaky round ears, but you aren't far off. What is your name?'

'Noosh.'

'Bless you. Now, what is your name?'

'Noosh.'

The Truth Pixie frowned. 'Bless you . . . You are quite a sneezy elf. I don't want elf snot on my carpet.'

'No. I'm not sneezing. My name is Noosh. That is my name.'

'Oh. Oh. I am so sorry. It must be horrible to be called something so stupid. My name is Truth Pixie. Much simpler.'

Noosh did her best to smile and not look upset. She

noticed a little brown mouse in the corner of the room.

'You have a mouse?'

The Truth Pixie nodded. She explained it was Maarta. The great-great-great-great-great-granddaughter of a mouse Father Christmas had known very well back when he was just an ordinary child called Nikolas. The mouse had been Father Christmas's only friend, and had accompanied him to the Far North and here to Elfhelm. Miika's great-great-great-great-great-granddaughter looked very much like him. She was nibbling on some cinnamon cake.

'Hello, Maarta,' said Noosh.

The mouse ignored her.

'She normally likes elves,' explained the Truth Pixie. 'So it must just be you.'

Noosh told herself not to be offended. 'Do you know anything about why the trolls attacked us last year?'

The Truth Pixie looked out of her little window, past the pines, up the hill towards the Troll Valley.

She suddenly looked a bit worried. She tried to lie.

'N . . .' She tried again. 'Nnnn . . .' She

tried to say no one more time. 'Nnnnnnnn . . . Yes, I do!' And the Truth Pixie slapped her hand over her mouth, knowing she'd said too much.

'Well, why was it? What were they angry at?'

The Truth Pixie frowned, and desperately tried to stop talking. 'They had been brainwashed.'

'Brainwashed? Who by?'

'By pixies. Some pixies. You understand there are different types of pixies, don't you?'

'Yes,' said Noosh. 'I know there are a few different types, but not all of them.'

The Truth Pixie explained in detail, hoping this would stop any further questions.

In addition to the Truth Pixie there was a Fear Pixie who lived all by herself, in a treehouse. She was scared of heights, so she never came down from the treehouse. (And no one knew why, if she was so scared of heights, she would have chosen to live in a treehouse in the first place.)

There were also Flying Story Pixies – of course, Noosh knew about these. She knew, even as the Truth Pixie was telling her, that they lived nowhere in particular, and had wings (unlike most pixies) and flew around the pixie area, Troll Valley, and sometimes even around Elfhelm, telling stories. They were the most miniature of all pixies. 'Oh, and then there is the Lie Pixie, who I didn't used to get on with at all. But I'm warming to him. He gives the best compliments.' But even though there were other pixies, Father Christmas was only really friends with the Truth Pixie, because a Truth Pixie is the only kind of pixie you can really trust.

'So, what do you know about what happened last Christmas Eve?'

'I really shouldn't say. I've said enough . . .' she blurted, almost in tears.

'Tell me what you know,' Noosh asked, her eyes staring fixedly at the pixie's delicate face.

The Truth Pixie sighed. She was now exhausted from all these impossible attempts to lie. She just couldn't do it. 'It was the Flying Story Pixies.'

'What? How?'

'Well, trolls are stupid. They are big and angry, but they don't know how to *think*. And pixies are the opposite. We are small and mischievous and think all the time. For instance, I've had three thousand, four hundred and eighty-two thoughts since I started this sentence. And Flying Story Pixies are the biggest thinkers of the lot. That is why they have wings. They had so many thoughts and imaginings that wanted to fly out of them that they ended up *actually flying*. And they can get inside other people's thoughts. They can . . . Can we talk about something else now? Can we talk about Maarta? Look how cute she is. Look at her. The way she eats the crumbs . . .'

But Noosh had more questions. 'What has this got to do with what happened last Christmas Eve?'

The Truth Pixie rolled her eyes. 'Well, the problem with Flying Story Pixies is that they chatter a lot. To themselves . . . And I hear them talking. And they got in their heads that it would be a bad idea for Christmas to happen.'

'Why?' wondered Noosh, scribbling all this down in her notebook. 'What have they got against Christmas?'

The Truth Pixie smiled. She liked this question. Because she could truthfully say, 'I don't know . . .'

'Could someone have put them up to it?'

'I don't know,' the pixie chirped. 'Listen,

Atishoo, I've got places to go . . . people to see . . . crackers to pull . . .'

'My name's not Atishoo. It's Noosh.'

'Whatever.'

Noosh looked at her watch. The hour hand was inching closer to the hour of Night.

'And this year? There have been reports in Elfhelm of noises under the ground. Do you think we should be worried?'

'I've heard nothing,' said the Truth Pixie, and she was now so frustrated she stood up and walked over to Noosh and reached up and pinched her hard on the nose. Even though pixies have small thin fingers they have a tight grip.

'Ow! What are you doing?' asked Noosh, her eyes watering with pain.

'I'm sorry. I've just always wanted to pinch an elf's nose. I don't know why. Do you want to pull a cracker?'

'Erm, no, but thanks very much, Truth Pixie,' said Noosh. 'I am going to go to the Troll Valley, and I will try to see a Flying Story Pixie and get some more facts.'

'Flying Story Pixies won't give you facts. They're allergic to facts. And the trolls will probably give you a horrible death.'

Now Noosh didn't want this conversation to carry on and felt an urgent need to get out of the too-small house. 'Well, thank you, Truth Pixie. This has been very enlightening. See you again.'

The Truth Pixie laughed her high-pitched squeal of a laugh. 'I doubt it!' she said. 'Where you are going!'

And Noosh smiled politely, said goodbye to the Truth Pixie and her mouse, and stooped out of the door, and back into the snow-covered hills, westwards to Troll Valley.

A Woman Called Mary

There is no Christmas in the workhouse,' Mrs Sharpe had said to Amelia. 'And no chitter chatter. There is only work from morning until night. Look. Look at these girls! They never speak. That will be you in a week. Silence is godliness.'

'Never,' said Amelia.

'Oh, you'll see. I have assured Mr Creeper you will have a deeply unpleasant time here. For the good of your own soul.'

That was last year. And Amelia was still in the workhouse three hundred and sixty-five days later. They had been the longest and most miserable days of her life. The life before that time seemed unreal to her now. It was like someone else's life. One she'd read about in a story somewhere. Amelia missed her mother and Captain Soot and she had to quietly beg her eyes not to leak tears.

She had been working for Mrs Sharpe in the laundry room. The laundry room was full of women and girls with blank faces who looked like they'd had the life sucked out of them. They folded clothes or washed them in sinks or squeezed them dry through a mangle.

There was no easy job in the laundry, but turning the mangle was generally considered the toughest.

A mangle was a machine that dried and flattened wet clothes. You fed the wet things between two wooden rollers then turned a heavy iron crank by hand to push the washing through.

It was so hard turning the crank it made Amelia's whole body ache, and Mrs Sharpe often stood behind her, barking comments. Amelia never knew if Mrs Sharpe was really properly horrid, or if she was just terrified of Mr Creeper.

'Come on, slowcoach. We haven't got all century,' Mrs Sharpe would say. And then Mr Creeper would walk into the room with his hands behind his back as if he was an emperor inspecting soldiers rather than a man inspecting a pile of pressed clothes.

'Not good enough,' he said. 'I want to see a significant improvement after lunch.'

But no matter how hard Amelia worked,

turning the crank as fast as she could, it was *never* enough for Mr Creeper, and if the pile of washing wasn't large enough he would ban her from the evening meal and keep her working till midnight.

It was lonely in the workhouse and Amelia had no friends. In fact no one had any friends in Creeper's Workhouse. Fear – that was the trouble. Everyone was scared. But fear was pointless. Amelia had run out of fear. Instead, she was angry.

She felt the anger rise up inside her chest like heat in a chimney.

She realised that this world, and everything in it, belonged to men. Except Queen Victoria. The only way to be female in this world, Amelia thought angrily, was to have a crown on your head. Because really the world was run by men. Cruel, unthinking men who didn't and would never care about the wishes and hopes of a ten-year-old girl like her. Men like Officer Pry. Men like Mr Creeper. Men who thought they were doing good but who were really doing harm. And yes, even Father Christmas. Yes, especially *him*. Father Christmas had made children believe in magic when actually a lot of life was very unmagical. What could be crueller than giving people hope in a hopeless world? Father Christmas didn't really care. He had just been showing off one Christmas. No. No one cared.

No one cared that she was so hungry she could have fainted. But when she was in the dinner hall, with all the girls and old women (boys ate separately), she would look at the grey slop being served by the kitchen maids and suddenly feel not so hungry.

There had been one girl, Emily, who whispered to her in the dormitory, but she had left the workhouse when she was sixteen, two weeks after Amelia had arrived. 'Always get your slop from Mary, the maid with the bun in her hair, the plump one,' Emily had whispered on Amelia's second night.

And the next day Amelia had seen the kitchen maids in a line over their saucepans, putting the grey sloppy liquid into the battered tin bowls that the girls and women held out. She spotted Mary instantly. She was the only one who was smiling. She had a round, rosy-cheeked face. She looked like an apple that had turned into a human.

So Amelia approached Mary and held out her bowl.

"'Ello, my dear. You're new, ain't you?'

Amelia nodded. The woman could see the sadness in Amelia's face.

'You look after yourself, all right?'

'Thanks,' mumbled Amelia, and she sat back down to discover that, yes, slop was *slightly* less disgusting with sugar in it. And she kept looking at Mary's face because it was kind, and warm, and it made a tiny spark of hope glow inside her like a lonely star in a dark, dark galaxy.

Over the year Mary would whisper little titbits about her life, sugaring the boredom of the workhouse with her own story. She had been at the workhouse since it opened. Mr Creeper had needed five hundred people to be at the workhouse for it to get its licence, so he had gone around the streets of London, and found Mary sleeping on a bench next to Tower Bridge, surrounded by pigeons. He had promised her warmth and food and a good life, and that hadn't happened. But even when there had been a chance for Mary to leave the workhouse she hadn't taken it. She had decided to stay, because, as she said, 'If there was a chance to make you poor young 'uns a little less miserable then I thought I'd 'ang around and sugar the slop.'

But even with the tiny comforts there wasn't a single second of the day that Amelia hadn't dreamt of one thing.

Escape.

She dreamt of leaving this horrid place and seeing Captain Soot again and running away to the countryside. Or anywhere that wasn't Creeper's Workhouse. And every single minute of every single day, she waited, like a cat watching a bird, for the right moment to strike.

Four Cheers for Father Christmas!

ather Christmas stood beside the infinity sack in front of all the elves in the Toy Workshop for the last time that year. Many of the elves were standing on tables. Some were holding the last toys they'd made that year, ready to drop them in the sack.

'Well, elves, you have done yourselves proud,' Father Christmas said, keeping an eye on the clock at the back of the room.

Everyone clapped and cheered. Bobbette the bubblemaker blew bubbles. Windy the whistlemaker blew a whistle. Dimple the prank toymaker sat down on a whoopee cushion. Bella the joke writer laughed. And Clementine the orange-haired satsuma grower fainted with excitement.

'Ho ho ho,' laughed Father Christmas.

'You did us proud more like,' said Humdrum, pushing his glasses further up his nose. Humdrum didn't like speaking in public, as a rule, but he'd got a bit carried away in the moment. His face was now as red as Father Christmas's outfit. He desperately tried to think of something funny or witty or heartfelt to say but he wasn't good with words, especially the words you say in front of people so instead he said, 'Three cheers for F-F-F-Father Christmas!'

The elves did four cheers because in elf arithmetic you always have to add one for good luck.

'Everything is going according to plan,' said Father Christmas. 'And not so much as a rumble from below the ground.'

As Father Christmas spoke a bell dinged and donged.

Father Topo, who had been standing near Father Christmas's side, went to open the door. It was the elf children from the kindergarten along with their teacher, Mother Loka.

Father Christmas laughed, because the sight of children always cheered him up. 'Ho ho ho. Hello, children! Do come in! There are lots of leftover toys for you to choose from!'

The children in their multi-coloured tunics and with beaming faces filed into the room, their little clogs clip-clopping on the floor. But then Humdrum began to panic. Father Topo saw his face, and realised what the problem was. Father Topo whispered into Mother Loka's ear, 'Where's Little Mim?'

Mother Loka smiled. 'He's right here.'

'Brilliant,' said Father Topo, seeing one hundred and seventy-two elf children, none of whom were Little Mim.

Then Mother Loka gasped, realising that Little Mim really *wasn't* there.

Humdrum began to panic.

Father Topo looked at his watch. It was five minutes after Quite Late in the Day. Humdrum was already out of the door, running home to see if his son was there.

Father Christmas was looking at all this commotion but hadn't overheard.

'Anything wrong, Father Topo?'

'No, no,' said Father Topo. 'No, no, no. No problem. Though it is Quite Late in the Day, so it is about time you and your infinity sack made their way to Reindeer Field.' Father Topo forced a smile, trying to keep worry out of the air. 'Come on, the whole world is waiting.'

The New Sleigh

There was a giant parcel sitting in the middle of Reindeer Field. Kip and Bibi were standing next to it. Purple-haired Bibi was Head of Wrapping Presents in the workshop, and her last job of the year had been to wrap this present for Father Christmas. Bibi, with her bow in her hair and her belt made of ribbon, looked like a parcel herself, and smiled excitedly at Father Christmas.

It was very nice wrapping paper, thought Father Christmas, as he walked across the snowy field. Sparkly silver stars against a shiny background with a bright red bow. Even the reindeer seemed impressed.

A huge crowd of excited elves had gathered. Everyone was wearing their favourite tunics. Most of these tunics were bright green or red. Father Vodol's was black. Kip's was a grey tunic with words knitted on the front. They said: 'NEVER EAT YELLOW SNOW.'

'Well, I wasn't expecting a present,' Father

Christmas laughed, and unwrapped it in wild bursts, the paper flying as the crowd cheered.

And there it was.

A new sleigh.

'It looks amazing,' said Father Christmas, because it did. Bright red, with sleek silver runners, and a polished wooden interior. It was twice the size of the last sleigh and there were more gadgets and dials on the dashboard too.

Father Christmas climbed in and sat on the luxury leather seat.

'Very nice indeed.'

Kip ran through everything in his low sleepy voice. 'There's the compass, that's your altitude gauge to show how high you are, that at the back is the propulsion unit . . .'

Father Christmas pointed at a strange curved object with a wire connecting it to the rest of the sleigh.

'That is the telephone,' said Kip. 'It lets you talk to the Toy Workshop HQ while you are in the air. I just invented it.'

'Telephone?'

'Yes. Well, I first called it a Tell-Elf-Home, but everyone kept on saying it wrong so now it is a telephone. What do you think?'

(Now, reader, I know what you are thinking. You are thinking, but hey, wait a minute, we're in 1841 and the telephone wasn't invented until 1849 by a young Italian man called Antonio Meucci, and a similar concept was later patented by Alexander Bell. Yes? Well, what you never actually hear is that both Antonio and Alexander were in fact *given* their telephones for Christmas, by Father Christmas the year after this one, and that the very first ever telephone was invented by this slightly forlorn elf in the grey tunic.)

'A telephone!' said Father Christmas. 'What a marvellous thing.'

And then he saw the most amazing thing of all, right on the dashboard. It was a glass semi-sphere sticking out of the woodwork. And inside were little clouds of green and violet and pink light swirling slowly around and through each other, like beautiful dancing ghosts.

'Wow,' said Father Christmas. 'An in-built Barometer of Hope. Well done, Kip. Well done indeed. Thank you so much for my Christmas present!'

He thought this new sleigh would make a great Christmas story for the *Daily Snow* so he looked around for Noosh, who was usually in Reindeer Field at this time of day. He scanned the crowd near the reindeer, but no, she wasn't there. She was nowhere among those smiling excited faces.

Even Father Vodol was smiling.

'Father Vodol, have you seen Noosh?'

Father Vodol scratched his beard nervously. 'I gave her the day off.'

'Oh,' said Father Christmas, and he had a feeling that something was wrong, or at least *not quite right*.

But then he looked at the shining sleigh and the eight reindeer and the happy crowd and he was excited again and he took a big breath and said to the crowd: 'THIS IS GOING TO MAKE UP FOR LAST YEAR. IT WILL BE THE MOST AMAZING CHRISTMAS EVER!'

And the crowd seemed to agree.

The Bite

As Amelia heaved the mangle crank that afternoon in the dark laundry room, she remembered last Christmas. When her mother had died. When Father Christmas failed to arrive. And when all the hope had fallen out of the world. She thought about Captain Soot's desperate farewell miaow. All these thoughts went round and round like the handle she was turning.

Her thoughts were interrupted by the sound of Mrs Sharpe scraping her chair as she got up and the slam of the door as she left the room.

The other girls were busy filling up the huge wash tub with hot water. This was Amelia's chance. She sneaked out, hidden by the foggy steam of the laundry room. In the corridor she could hear voices and footsteps. She ran into the first empty room she could find and shut the door quietly behind her. She looked at the windows. They were high up, so she had to climb on a chair to unlock the rusty window latch and then use all her strength to try and open the heavy window. She wasn't thinking straight. She knew this wasn't much of a plan. The workhouse's main fireplace would have been a better idea, but there was no way of getting there without being noticed. Her arms were so sore and tired and empty from turning the mangle crank that even though she pushed and pushed, the window would not budge.

Oh, and then: 'WHAT DO YOU THINK YOU ARE DOING?'

Mr Creeper. He slammed his cane down and marched over to her.

'Get off me, you horrible raggabrash!' Amelia said. Mr Creeper's long skinny old hand was right there in front of her face as he reached up to lock the window. So she did something.

Something risky.

Something silly.

Something, she was sure, that Captain Soot would approve of.

She *bit* him.

That's right. Amelia bit into Mr Creeper's hand, pressing her teeth into his skin as hard as she could. And even though her arms didn't have any strength in them, it turned out that her teeth did.

'AAAAAAAAAAGGGGHHHH!!!' wailed Mr Creeper. 'YOU ANIMAL! SOMEBODY GET THIS MONSTROUS CHILD OFF ME!!!'

And within a moment or two Mrs Sharpe was pulling her off Mr Creeper, who was now staring at the bright red bite-mark imprinted on his skin.

'Well,' he said to Amelia, as she tried to fight free from Mrs Sharpe. 'Twelve months and she's still a wild animal! Still the same girl who kicked me last year! Just like your foolish father.'

'What do you know about my father?'

'I knew him as a boy. We grew up on the same street. He was a violent rat . . . He thought doing *this*,' he pointed at his broken crooked nose, 'was the same as standing on a cat's tail.'

Amelia smiled. She knew her dad was a hero.

'You're as stupid as him. Take her downstairs! To the basement! And lock her in the refractory cell! And KEEP HER THERE!'

And so Amelia was dragged downstairs by Mrs Sharpe and locked in a bare room with nothing but a hard bed and a chamber pot and a tiny barred window. She sat on the cold stone floor and let the tears fall like rain out of her eyes and felt every last drop of hope leave her body.

The child who once had the most hope had now almost completely run out. And so, at exactly the same time, in the sky just south of Elfhelm, the Northern Lights lost some of their glow.

A Crash Landing

ather Christmas rose up on his sleigh, through the cold night air, and already – compared to last year – this was a miracle. He supposed that everything was going to plan because there had been no troll attack. He smiled, looking at the world below, and the reindeer bottoms in front. But he had to admit, the sleigh's Barometer of Hope was not glowing as much as he would have liked.

'Can you see the lights yet, Blitzen? Can you see them, Donner? Any of you?'

Blitzen nodded, without looking around.

Yes, there they were. Rippling curtains of pale green and violet spread across the air.

'Right into them, deers!' Father Christmas told the reindeer. 'Right into the light . . . This is SO EXCITING!'

And his whole body tingled with joyous magic as he travelled through the lights, seeing nothing but green and violet *luminescence* (which was his third favourite word, after *magic* and *chocolate*). He felt so warm and happy and full of confidence that he could do anything, even stop time itself.

He knew, though, that if he was to do *that* he had to be quick. With the coloured lights all around he looked at the clock in the sleigh. It was only a few seconds after the Beginning of Night. He pressed the little button right in the centre of the clock. The button that said 'STOP'.

And Father Christmas watched the second hand stop, and go no further.

'And you *stay* there,' he told that second hand.

Snow hung motionless in the air. They passed a large white-and-black bird that was totally still, high in the sky, with wings outstretched. An arctic goose, frozen in time. When Father Christmas had delivered all his presents this goose, along with the rest of the world, would carry on moving, as if nothing had happened. Birds would carry on flying. Snowflakes would carry on falling. Children would wake up and see their presents in their stockings. Hope would be restored.

He then spoke the first child's name. The first child he ever visited.

'Amelia Wishart,' he said, remembering two Christmases ago. The girl who had sent him a letter. The letter that had flown through the air last December and landed on the south side of Big Mountain. According to Pip, the letter catcher who had been on duty, no letter had flown further up the mountain. The letter he'd had in his pocket ever since.

And the compass shifted, south-westwards, which told him which direction to steer. So he tugged on the reins with his right hand, as the propulsion unit display glowed an intense red. The speedometer pointed to 'VERY FAST INDEED', the altitude gauge read, 'IN THE CLOUDS' and Father Christmas and the reindeer sped through the nineteen hundred and eighty-two miles to the city of London.

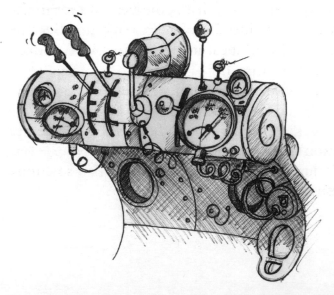

'Ho ho ho!' said Father Christmas, laughing to himself with sheer joy as he flew over Finland and Sweden and Denmark. Passing over houses he would visit later in the night or, rather, the same time in the night. He was determined to begin with London, with Amelia, as that would be lucky. And she had written him that letter – quite an important letter. And he needed to try and give this girl the happiest Christmas ever. As he flew he decided to talk to the reindeer. He often spoke to the reindeer. He was, after all, the author of one of Elfhelm's bestselling books *The Reindeer Whisperer*.

'Shall I tell you some jokes?'

The reindeer galloped faster, as if the jokes were something they could run away from. Father Christmas didn't get the hint.

'All right . . . What is the best present in the world? Any ideas? No? A broken drum. Because you just can't beat it! Do you get it? A broken drum! Ho ho ho!'

He looked down. They were over water now.

'Hello, sea!' he shouted down. Then he chuckled, thinking of another joke. 'The sea didn't answer. It just waved . . . Do you get it? It just *waved*. Because of waves. It's so funny, isn't it?'

The reindeer said nothing.

'Do you want another one? I've got more. Have you heard the one about the pixie whose head got stuck up an elf's . . .'

Father Christmas stopped. Everything was still as it should be. The sleigh was still flying. The reindeer were still galloping through the air. He still felt happy.

But.

But, but, but, *but*.

Something was happening to the Barometer of Hope. He tapped it. Then gave it a bit of a bash. But there was no doubt about it – the lights *were* fading.

'Oh dear,' said Father Christmas. 'Not again.'

The altitude reading had now slipped lower to 'BELOW THE CLOUDS'. Father Christmas called to his reindeer.

'Higher! We're not in London yet!'

The reindeer tried their best but they didn't seem able to rise any higher.

'Blitzen? Are you struggling? Blitzen, if you are and finding this hard, raise your head.'

Blitzen raised his head.

Father Christmas picked up that thing called a telephone and said, 'Hello?'

And a worried voice came back. 'Hello?'

It was Father Topo.

'Oh, hello, Father Topo. I was just checking that nothing is wrong in Elfhelm.'

Father Topo cleared his throat on the other end of the line. 'Wrong? No. No. Everything is quite all right. Why do you ask?'

'I'm just having a bit of a problem with the reindeer. We don't seem to be able to fly high enough in the sky. And the Barometer of Hope is looking a bit, erm, unhopeful.' Father Christmas knew that if hope levels were down it meant one of two things: trouble in the human world or trouble back in Elfhelm. Or both.

Father Topo coughed uncertainly. 'Everything is fine, Father Christmas. You just carry on your way.'

And Father Christmas saw the dim lights of London up ahead.

'All right, Father Topo,' Father Christmas said as the sleigh lowered.

And Father Topo said, 'Just be careful out there.'

Father Christmas looked over the side of his sleigh. He had forgotten how *big* London was – all those moonlit buildings and churches that seemed to go on for ever with the River Thames snaking through the middle. Then his stomach felt light and tickly, and he saw the reindeer struggling again.

'We're not at Haberdashery Road yet!'

He saw Blitzen turn around and give Father Christmas a desperate look.

'Oh, my deers! Come on! You can do it! Stay in the air!'

He looked at the altitude reading. It said 'WORRYINGLY LOW BUT YOU SHOULD BE ALL RIGHT'. And then seconds later it said 'NO, ACTUALLY, THIS IS TOO LOW. YOU'D BETTER PANIC'.

Father Christmas looked for somewhere to land. It had to be somewhere close. And it had to be somewhere flat and large and out of view. Ideally a roof. But what roof would be big enough?

And then he saw it.

The largest house ever.

It had a hundred windows, all tall and neat like soldiers standing to attention. Actually, now you mention it, there *were* real soldiers standing outside the gates, wearing tall black furry bearskin hats. It was so large. It was larger than the Toy Workshop. It was larger than any building in the whole of Finland. It was perfect.

'All right, reindeer,' he shouted, 'we're coming in to land. Donner, Blitzen, you see that roof? That's where we're headed. The rest of you, don't slow till we get there.'

But they *were* slowing. And the sleigh was tilting too. And then he noticed something. The tall-hatted soldiers weren't standing to attention now. They were aiming their guns at the sleigh.

Bang!

A shot sounded. And a bullet whizzed by.

Bang!

Another one.

Making a hole in the side of the sleigh.

'No, no, no!'

This was bad news for two reasons. First, Father Christmas didn't like the idea of him or his reindeer getting shot. And second, for the soldiers to be moving and shooting, it meant time must be moving forward.

And yes – look – the whole of London was in motion. With horses and carts and night-time churchgoers.

He looked at the clock in the sleigh. It was still only the Beginning of Night but he could see the second hand was now ticking forward.

He jabbed the 'STOP' button but nothing happened. He noticed the chamber in the Barometer of Hope was now just empty glass.

'Uh-oh,' he mumbled as he and the sleigh dipped fast through the air.

He saw the roof they were aiming at. It was too high now. They weren't going to reach it. They needed more magic.

'Jingle bells,' he sang, 'jingle bells, jingle all the way.'

Bang!

As the bullet went through Father Christmas's sack, chocolate coins burst out in a shower of gold.

'Oh, what fun it is to ride in a . . .'

Father Christmas closed his eyes and prepared for impact.

Smash!

But instead of hitting the stone wall the reindeer's hooves made contact with a large window. Wood and glass splintered and burst into smithereens in front of them.

'Oh, mudfungle,' said Father Christmas, using the worst pixie swearword he knew as he sped through the window behind the deer.

Crash!

The reindeer skidded along the floor of a

long room and screeched to a halt in a tangle of hooves on a plush patterned carpet before piling into a table. Father Christmas tipped out of the sleigh. He hit the wall. Then a giant vase on the table wobbled, then tottered, then teetered. Then finally fell. Right on top of Father Christmas's head, before breaking into a thousand pieces.

The sound of a scream rang out. But it wasn't coming from Father Christmas.

A Royal Guest

lbert!' shouted the voice.

It was a young woman. She was wearing a long white nightdress and sitting in a very grand four-poster bed, in a room with the plushest softest carpet Father Christmas had ever trodden on (and he had trodden on a *lot* of carpets). She was reading something that looked a bit like a magazine. Father Christmas was less interested in what the young woman was reading and more interested in what she was wearing on her head.

A *crown*.

Gold, jewel-encrusted and dazzling.

And she was wearing it sitting up *in bed*.

Queen Victoria.

The Queen of England. The most powerful woman in the world. And he had just smashed into her bedroom.

'ALBEEEERRRRRTTT!' She had a very loud voice for a small woman. 'Get the guards. And bring your gun! We have an intruder! A

big fat Frenchman with a beard has just crashed into the royal bedroom with the help of some flying devil-horses. One is most alarmed INDEED!'

'They're actually reindeer. And I'm not, um, French. Let me explain.'

A tall thin man with a baby face and a wispy moustache that seemed to be made out of cotton appeared. He walked into the room wearing striped pyjamas and carrying a rifle. He pointed the gun at Father Christmas.

'It's all right, lambkin. I've g-g-got him.'

'Blow his head off, Albert! Be a man for once!'

Father Christmas noticed that Albert's hands were shaking. And so was the gun.

'Listen,' said Father Christmas. 'I am very sorry about all this. And we'll clean up all the mess.'

'Oh, please don't worry about the mess,' said Albert. 'We have servants.'

Queen Victoria looked at Albert crossly. 'Albert! What are you doing? Why are you being so, so . . . *royal* about this?'

'I *am* royal, honeycheeks.'

'But he's an intruder. Very possibly French.'

'Technically Finnish, with a sprinkling of elf,

but that came later,' added Father Christmas helpfully.

Queen Victoria glared at her husband, her cheeks red with fury. 'While you were hanging pretty baubles on that silly tree you got from Norway this hairy beast flew in with his devil-horses and tried to kidnap me!'

Father Christmas was upset by this. His own father may have been a kidnapper, but he certainly wasn't. 'I wasn't trying to kidnap you.'

Just as he said this, Blitzen decided this would be the perfect time to go to the loo. Right there on the thick carpet. A big steaming pile of brown reindeer dung.

'Oh no,' wailed the Queen. 'One of the devil-horses has done a stinky on the royal carpet!'

Father Christmas sighed at Blitzen. 'I'm really sorry about that.'

'Shoot him, Albert. Shoot the hairy man. And then shoot his beastly devil-horses!'

The rifle shook in Albert's hands. 'All right. All right. I'll do it. I can do it, can't I?'

'Of course you can, pumpkin,' the Queen said, a bit softer now. 'Come on, my sweet German prince. Shoot him in his big fat belly. Actually, it might bounce off. Aim for the face.'

'It feels wrong, you know, doing it here.'

Queen Victoria looked cross again. 'Well, I'll have to call Baroness Lehzen . . . BARONESS! BARONESSSSSSSSS!'

Prince Albert rolled his eyes. 'Not the house dragon!'

Then a very large old lady with broad shoulders, thick arms, a hairy chin and a long black dress came in. She looked like she was chewing a wasp.

'Vot iz it, Your Highness?' she asked, in a German voice.

'There has been an intruder and he needs to be shot. Albert! Give the Baroness the gun right now.'

But the Baroness didn't need a gun. She walked over to Father Christmas and pinched his nose. Then twisted it. Then pushed it. Father Christmas had never known pain like it. He held his nose as he fell back onto the floor.

The Baroness turned to the Queen. 'Many years ago, before I voz your governess, I used to partake in a little street-fighting. The other girl wrestlers knew me as zee Horror of Hannover.'

Father Christmas watched in, yes, horror as the woman leant over and picked him up by his red coat and trousers. She started to swing him around in a circle. Albert put his hand over his eyes.

'Smash him, Baroness!' said Queen Victoria, clapping excitedly. 'Throw him out of the window!'

And the reindeer watched in horror as Baroness Lehzen spun like a spinning top, faster and faster and faster, until with a great roar she let go. Father Christmas took to the air for the second time this evening, and flew out of the same window he'd entered minutes before.

'Auf Wiedersehen, you kidnapping French swine,' she shouted, with a little grunting laugh in her voice.

Dasher to the Rescue!

ather Christmas was flying through the air and falling, as fast as a plum pudding, towards the ground. But wait, what was that flash of shadow heading fast towards him?

It was Dasher! The fastest of all reindeer. He dived down and curved back underneath Father Christmas, just before he landed on the ground.

Bang!

The soldiers were shooting again so Dasher carried Father Christmas back up to the room. When they got there, Father Christmas saw Queen Victoria now holding the large rifle and she was pointing it directly at him.

'How do they do that?' she asked.

Father Christmas was staring at the gun. 'Do what?'

'The flying horse-devils. How do they fly?'

Father Christmas didn't like it when she called the reindeer horse-devils, because the reindeer were sensitive creatures, especially

Prancer, and they wouldn't like being called names.

'They are reindeer. They have nothing to do with horses or devils. They are very special creatures. And they fly because of magic. There is magic in the air because it is Christmas. But there needs to be more magic in the air. That's why we crashed into your window. The flying was going a bit wrong . . .'

'So who the dickens *are* you?'

'I'm Father Christmas!'

'Father Christmas? Who's that? Never heard of you.'

'I have, sugarplum,' said Albert nervously, as if every word he spoke was made of porcelain. 'I heard about him from Henrik. You know? My Norwegian friend. The one I got the tree from. He's the man who went around the world on Christmas Eve giving presents to all the children, a couple of years ago.'

'Oh yes. I heard about

that. What a creepy thing to do! Sneaking into people's bedrooms.'

Father Christmas shook his head. 'I don't do any sneaking. You see, I stop time. Well, that's the idea. Using magic to give people hope, which, in turn, helps create magic.'

This made Queen Victoria cross. And her cross-face was one of the crossest cross-faces in human history. 'By smashing into Buckingham Palace? We've only just moved in. Look at the mess you've all made.'

Prince Albert raised his hand.

'Permission to speak,' said the Queen.

'I was just going to point out that we do have two hundred and fifty-two other bedrooms, feather-cheeks.'

'That is beside the point. Baroness, give him a slap!'

The Baroness gave poor Prince Albert a sharp slap across the face.

'It was an accident,'

said Father Christmas, talking about the window. 'I am very sorry.'

Two soldiers from outside had now arrived in the bedroom too, a bit out of breath after running up the stairs. 'At your service, Your Majesty!'

The Queen nodded at the soldiers and had one more question for Father Christmas. 'You do know who you're talking to, don't you?'

'Yes. You are the Queen of England.'

'Yes,' said the Queen. 'Technically the Queen of the United Kingdom of Great Britain and Ireland, and Head of the British Empire, which covers most places. So you could say one is the most important person in the whole world.'

'Shall we kill the intruder?' asked the soldiers.

'I really feel it would be bad form to kill Father Christmas,' said Albert.

'Shut up, Albert,' said Queen Victoria. And then she gave Father Christmas a long hard stare.

'How do we know you *are* Father Christmas?'

'The reindeer were flying. Surely that is proof of magic.'

'I suppose it is a bit strange,' said Queen Victoria. 'But lots of things are strange. Like fish. And belly buttons. And the poor. We should probably not shoot you though.'

Father Christmas was overjoyed. 'Oh, thank you. That is such a relief.'

'No. I will have you hanged instead.'

Father Christmas gulped. He needed to think of something. So he closed his eyes and he thought very deeply. He went into a kind of dream. He saw an unhappy eight-year-old girl who looked very like Queen Victoria. She was in a very lovely room, full of amazing things – a rocking horse, spinning tops, tea sets, a hundred dolls – but she was getting shouted at, by a woman with her hair in a bun. A younger Baroness Lehzen. 'I want my mummy,' the girl whimpered to her governess. 'Where is my mummy?'

'You are being VERY NAUGHTY, Victoria!' roared the Baroness. 'I have to train you to be a lady! You could be Queen one day.'

'But I don't want to be Queen!'

'Don't say that, or you won't get any presents for Christmas.'

'The only thing I want for Christmas is not to be Queen – never, ever, ever!'

And so Father Christmas opened his eyes,

and he said what he had just heard in his mind. 'The only thing you wanted for Christmas, when you were a little girl, was not to be Queen – *never, ever, ever.*'

Queen Victoria looked very, very sad. Very, very, very sad indeed. Maybe even sadder than that.

'How do you know that?'

'Because I am Father Christmas.'

She laid the gun down and gently flapped her hands, telling the guards and Baroness Lehzen to leave. When the last guard had left the room she became lost in thought, as Blitzen began nibbling on the posh curtains. 'I wasn't a happy child, you know? Everyone expected me to act a certain way, because I was going to become Queen. It is a lot of pressure, when everyone expects you to be something important. Do you understand?'

Father Christmas knew the feeling.

'Completely,' said Father Christmas. 'Yes. I really do.'

'I had lots of toys, but there was no magic.'

Father Christmas felt like he wanted to cheer her up, so he started singing 'Jingle Bells'.

'What are you doing?' she asked him.

'I'm singing "Jingle Bells".'

'Why?'

'To cheer you up.'

Queen Victoria burst out laughing. Albert looked concerned. 'Darling, one of the horse-devils is eating the curtains.'

'He's not a horse-devil,' said the Queen. 'He's a *reindeer*.'

And then she smiled at Father Christmas. And Father Christmas smiled back.

The Royal Seal of Approval

Queen Victoria apologised to Father Christmas. She really was very sorry.

'To give magic to children, what a wonderful thing,' she said.

'The trouble,' said Father Christmas, 'is that the magic is not very magic at the moment.' He pointed at the smashed window and the billowing curtains to illustrate his point. 'Last year, there was no magic at all. Christmas didn't happen. And Christmas *has* to happen this year . . .

'I had nothing when I was a child,' sighed Father Christmas. 'Well, I had a doll made out of a turnip. And a sleigh. But it wasn't like this one.'

He pointed at the large red sleigh and noticed a small tiny flicker of light appear inside the Barometer of Hope.

The Queen had more to say. 'I'd have loved to have believed in magic. To know that some things can't be explained. To have some mystery. That would have made everything better. You see, there was no mystery in my life and there never has been. Everything I've done was planned *in advance* and that can be as dull as a London fog.'

Queen Victoria sailed gracefully across the room in her nightdress to reach a small antique table, the colour of chestnut, and sat down at it, to write a note. And once she had finished writing, she picked up a wooden stamp and pressed it down on the piece of paper. It made a splodgy red mark on the paper with a picture of a crown in it.

'The Royal Seal of Approval,' she said with pride. 'There,' she said. 'If you get into any trouble, just give them this. Show this letter to anyone and they will know it was written by the real me.'

Father Christmas looked at the letter. It wasn't a very long letter. The letter said:

'Dear Whoever You Are, Be nice to this man. Yours faithfully, Queen Victoria.'

Father Christmas felt a warm feeling in his belly. 'Thank you. It's nice to have friends in high places.'

She gave a small smile. 'Likewise.'

Dear Whoever You Are
Be nice to this man.

Yours faithfully

Queen Victoria

'What would you like for Christmas?' he asked her.

Queen Victoria thought for a very long time. 'India would be nice.'

'India?' said Father Christmas. 'I think India is a bit *big*. It seems a bit . . . wrong to give somebody a country.'

'Well, India will be mine one day. I assure you. But in the meantime a teapot would do very nicely.'

'I think we have a spare,' Father Christmas said.

So he went over to the infinity sack. And stuck his arm inside and wished for the right teapot — a white one with a pretty blue pattern of willow trees on it — and sure enough he felt the smooth cold china of a teapot handle against his palm. He pulled it out.

'Yes!' said the Queen. 'That is the exact one I wanted.'

Father Christmas nodded. 'I have a lot more

presents to deliver,' he said as he settled into the sleigh and took the reins.

'But what if you crash again?' the Queen said, actually looking a little bit concerned.

Father Christmas saw there was now a little bit of hope in the barometer. Maybe this meeting with the Queen had been enough to put some hope back in the air. Father Christmas pressed the clock's stop button and, yes, it worked again.

Kind of.

Queen Victoria stopped moving. She became as still as the oil paintings on the walls. But then started moving again, very slowly.

'All right, my deers. Time has slowed but not quite stopped. We better get on our way and just hope we're too fast and they're too slow for anyone to see us in the sky.'

And the reindeer took off, galloping through the broken window and into that London sky. A little wobbly, but they made it, safely flying over churches and houses and the round onion dome of Saint Paul's Cathedral, and past incredibly slow-flying pigeons until they all landed on the slate-tiled roof of 99 Haberdashery Road.

There was a man and a woman walking arm

in arm on the street below. They were almost still. But not quite. The man was smoking a pipe. He was taking it out of his mouth in extreme slow motion. Then Prancer, standing a little awkwardly on the roof, slipped on a tile and the tile became unstuck, and then it slid, very slowly, over the other tiles.

Father Christmas leant forward inside the sleigh and repeatedly pressed the stop button but the tile was still moving.

'Oh dear.'

Time had to stop – stop *completely*. It couldn't just *stutter* or *slow down*. There were 227,892,951 children he had to give presents to. That was a lot of children. So yes. Time had to stop.

What he didn't know – but was about to find out – was that at least part of the answer lay at the bottom of this chimney. The chimney he was standing above and stepping inside, and climbing down simply by wishing. And as he travelled through it, he noticed, right at the top, fingerprints in the soot. They indicated the smallness of a child.

Hmmm, thought Father Christmas. And that small hum of a thought was about to grow into something very worrying indeed.

The Girl with a Beard

omething *was* wrong.
Father Christmas could sense that, even before he saw the bed.

Then he did see the bed.

And he gasped.

Amelia had grown.

Father Christmas knew that she was ten years old and he knew that there was a big difference between eight years old and ten but she was now the size of the entire bed. And she had a belly as large as Father Christmas's. And she was snoring like a pig with a cold.

He looked around.

The place looked the same as it had two years ago.

There were bare damp walls with paint peeling off them. There was water dripping in from the ceiling, because of the leaky roof. And where was the cat? There was no sign or trace or smell of the black cat that had been sleeping on her bed the last time he'd been here.

And there was a bottle by Amelia's bed.

A whisky bottle.

Did ten-year-old girls drink whisky these days?

Then he saw something out of the window. A small shadow falling fast – in real time – and reaching the ground with a *smash!*

Father Christmas saw, from the glow of the moon, the remnants of the smashed roof tile on the ground. The couple he had seen earlier were nowhere to be seen. Snow was falling.

A floorboard creaked.

Then Amelia sat up in bed and she had a beard as bushy as Father Christmas's, and as big, bristly and black as Father Vodol's. She looked about forty-nine.

'You're not Amelia.'

'What are you doing in my room?!' roared the man, who had a rough voice and looked (and smelled) like a pirate. The man picked up the empty whisky bottle and threw it at Father Christmas's head. Father Christmas ducked and the bottle smashed against the wall.

'Oh dear,' said Father Christmas. And then he reached in his sack for something the man might like. He pulled out an eye patch. 'You might like this,' Father Christmas told him. 'As it makes you look even more like a pirate.'

The man did not like this. 'I don't look

anything like a pirate. But you do. You look like a big red pirate.'

So Father Christmas found a batch of chocolate money in his sack.

'I'm Father Christmas. I'm not a thief or anything. Please take these.'

'Coins?' said the man.

'Made out of chocolate,' said Father Christmas. 'The very best elf-made chocolate.'

'Made out of chocolate? What a good idea!' said the man. He bit into one.

'You have to unwrap them,' Father Christmas explained.

'Oh yes. I see that.'

'I'm sorry I gave you a shock. Listen, are you Amelia's father?'

'Who's Amelia?'

'She lives here. I thought she lived here.'

The man had a think.

'Well, I've been here a year now. But the neighbours say the lady who was here before died . . . She had a girl, but I never knew what happened to her.'

Father Christmas gasped. He had a sinking feeling as he remembered Amelia's letter. The one she had sent before the Christmas that never happened.

'Right,' said Father Christmas. 'I see. Well. Thank you. And now I'll be on my way.'

And the man was surprised to see that, instead of heading out the door, Father Christmas headed towards the fireplace.

'How are you going to fit in there?'

'Magic,' said Father Christmas. 'Merry Christmas.'

And Father Christmas disappeared up the chimney that was clearly too small for a grown man to fit inside.

But then, near the top of the chimney, Father Christmas did get a bit stuck. His head was peeping out of the top. He felt like he was trapped tight in a giant's fist.

'Well, this is a bit embarrassing,' he said, as all the reindeer on the roof stared at him. Comet was laughing, fast little air clouds coming out of his nostrils.

'Comet, this really isn't funny.'

Blitzen carefully bowed his head for Father Christmas to grab hold of his antlers. He held tight as Blitzen walked slowly backwards.

Pop!

Father Christmas flew out of the chimney like a cork from a bottle. Luckily though, his grip on the antlers was so tight that he didn't fly too far. In fact, he just did one big somersault and landed on the reindeer's back.

'Thank you, Blitzen,' he said, giving Comet a bit of a glare. 'A good friend as always.'

Then he slid off Blitzen's back and walked delicately along the roof to the sleigh.

Father Christmas Makes a Decision

Now.

It was quite complicated.

The way the magic worked.

The Northern Lights, stopping time, flying through the air and everything.

It was dependent on many, many things. Maybe even many, many, *many* things.

To explain it in all its detail would take a lot of books. It would take seven thousand, four hundred and sixty-two books. And I would love to write them all but my fingers would drop off and I would get too hungry.

And anyway if you explain magic in too much detail it flies away. You know, like when you see a pretty butterfly and you want to get a better look so you go over to the butterfly and then the butterfly flies off and you can't see it at all.

(And if you didn't think that last sentence made sense, I should tell you that it absolutely did and you should read it again.)

But there are some things I *can* tell you. For one thing: Father Christmas was confused.

He knew there was something going on in Elfhelm. Something Father Topo wasn't telling him.

What he did know was that Amelia Wishart was missing. And Amelia Wishart was important. She was the first child. She was the one who had hoped the most that first ever Christmas. Hope was important. Hope was the main ingredient. But hope itself is another kind of complicated magic. Amelia was the one who had put enough magic in the air simply by *believing in it*. And this was before any child in the world had known about Father Christmas. She had believed. Not in him. But in possibility. In the kind of possibility that could mean something like delivering toys to every child on earth could actually happen.

'Right,' Father Christmas explained to the reindeer, on that roof. 'Look, I think we can save Christmas. But we need to find this girl. She will be somewhere in London. So . . . *I am going to find her.*'

Walking Among Humans

ather Christmas knew that reindeer on a roof could look a bit suspicious, especially with time moving at normal speed, so he took them on a very wonky flight to some snow-covered strawberry fields in a village called Hackney on the outskirts of town.

'Now, you deers, keep out of mischief! I won't be long. I can't be.'

So, Father Christmas walked into London. It was a rather strange experience. For one thing, it was so dull and dark.

Also nobody else was wearing a bright red suit, complete with bright red hat. The only hats around were black, except for some of the white bonnets worn by women coming out of carol services. Everyone dressed very drably. He took the bright red hat off and put it in his pocket.

There were no reindeer or sleighs either. And nothing smelled of gingerbread. Just smoke and dirt and horse poo.

'A world without magic,' he said to himself, 'can be a sad place.'

The other strange thing was that time kept on stopping and starting again. It was like the world was one big breaking machine that kept juddering off and on. Obviously, he wanted the world to stay still and out of time because then it would give him more chance to find Amelia *and* be able to deliver all the toys. He passed a church clock near Haberdashery Road which said it was now half past midnight. That was the hour of Very Very Late in elf time.

There weren't that many people about now. There was an old woman sitting on a bench. She had no teeth and milky eyes and was wearing a shawl. She was in the middle of feeding some pigeons. The pigeons stopped moving in mid-air. Then started. Then stopped.

Father Christmas went and sat down next to her while she was frozen in time, and when she came back to life she leant in with her onion breath and said, ''Ello, 'andsome!'

And he said hello and asked her about Amelia, but she had never heard of her and when she asked the pigeons they hadn't either.

It was a dark night and there was a thick

London fog too. So even when time was moving, things sort of appeared and disappeared. Men wobbling their way home from the pub singing Christmas songs. A rat catcher with his pockets full of rats. As Father Christmas walked on he saw a Christmas market. All the wheeled stalls were empty, except one. A chestnut seller. Father Christmas went over to her.

'Chestnuts?' the chestnut seller asked. She had a narrow face and a colourful knitted shawl. She scratched the shawl that covered her head. 'As much as you want for three farthings?'

Father Christmas gave her three chocolate coins. She stared at the coins.

'Chocolate,' he explained.

She opened it. And ate the chocolate. She closed her eyes and didn't speak for a little while because she was enjoying the chocolate so much.

'Oh, that is very nice chocolate.'

'I know. And it is also money.'

She laughed suspiciously. 'Where?'

'In the north.'

She thought. 'Manchester?'

'No. Further . . . Never mind. Listen, I don't mind about the chestnuts. I'm looking for a girl. Her name is Amelia Wishart. She's a . . .

er . . . family friend and she's gone missing. She has a black cat.'

'Well, she could be on the streets. If she's lucky.'

'Lucky? To live on the streets?'

Father Christmas remembered the three months when his Aunt Carlotta had made him sleep outside as a boy. And then how he had struggled to keep warm and fall asleep on his quest to the Far North. Those nights outside still gave him nightmares to this day.

'Or she might be dead of course? 'Ow old is she?'

'Ten.'

'Well, ten is a good age. Quite old round 'ere. She might have died of natural causes.'

'At *ten?!*'

'Dead's not the worst thing that can 'appen to a child round 'ere.'

Father Christmas really was confused now. And more than a little worried. 'Really? What's worse than death?'

Her face went paler than it already was (it was already pretty pale). Her nose twitched as if waiting for a sneeze that was never going to happen. And then her eyes became wide and full of horror.

'*The workhouse*,' she said.

Father Christmas frowned. 'What's a workhouse?'

'A terrible place. Terrible. Terrible.' She kept on saying 'terrible' for a while. 'They take the poor. I used to be there. They pretend they are doing you good. But they aren't. They aren't. They aren't . . . Managed to earn my way out. Took me years. Some aren't so lucky.'

'Which workhouse would she be in?'

'There's lots. Old Kent Road Workhouse. Gracechurch. Bread Street. Smith's Workhouse. Creeper's Workhouse. Allhallows Workhouse. Dowgate. Saint Mary-le-Bow. Jones's Workhouse . . .'

She gave a list of so many names Father Christmas didn't know where to start. 'But just hope she's in none of 'em.'

'All right,' said Father Christmas. 'I'll hope.'

Then a memory passed across the woman's face, like sun across a street.

'You say she had a black cat, Mister?'

'Yes. With a white tip at the end of its tail.'

The chestnut seller clapped her hands together. 'Wait a minute. Yes. There *was* a girl with a cat, now you come to mention it. A year to the day! She wanted to stay at my house. I felt so guilty saying no. But you see I 'ave a problem with cats and my house . . . well, you couldn't fit anything in there. Even a pixie would struggle.'

'I doubt that,' said Father Christmas. 'But do you know where she went?'

'She *was* worried about being sent to a workhouse.'

'Oh no.'

'So I sent 'er off to find Saint Paul's Cathedral. To 'ead to old Mrs Broadheart. Used to know 'er meself when I was in trouble as a young 'un. My name's Bessie by the way. Bessie Smith.'

She seemed to be waiting for Father Christmas to say his name but he didn't. 'And remind me. My magic isn't . . . I mean, my *memory* isn't what it was . . . Which way to Saint Paul's?'

And at that point she froze.

As still as anything. Just like the smoke from the cooking chestnuts. 'Thank you,' Father Christmas said, knowing she couldn't hear him, but he headed quickly off in the direction of her unmoving pointed finger, trying to get there before time started again.

The Cat

Outside the cathedral, he looked around for a sign of old Mrs Broadheart. There were quite a few old ladies now time had started moving again. In fact, they were the only people around. Apart from pigeons.

There was an old hunchbacked lady sitting on a bench.

'Are you Mrs Broadheart?'

She looked at Father Christmas with big, confused eyes. 'No. I'm a pigeon.'

'I'm pretty sure you're a human.'

And then the woman laughed so hard she fell off the bench and a pigeon flew down and landed on her face.

Then another old woman came over. Her face was wrinkled as a walnut. 'Ignore Janey. She's been drinking sherry. Well, it is Christmas.'

'Are you Mrs Broadheart?'

'Oh no,' she said. 'Mrs Broadheart's in prison.

Her and her gang of girl thieves got caught stealing Christmas puddings.'

Father Christmas nodded. A small worry entered his brain. But then he hurried it away. Amelia was no thief. 'I'm looking for a girl called Amelia. Amelia Wishart.'

'Doesn't ring a bell.'

And just as she said 'bell' the church bells began ringing and the old woman on the ground started laughing as the pigeon flew off her face.

Father Christmas went and sat down on another wooden bench, closer to the river. The ripples, outside of time, were waiting for hovering snowflakes to land and disappear.

The girl went missing over a year ago so she really could be anywhere. *A year ago! Maybe that was how hope was lost! Maybe that was how the troll attack was able to happen! And why the Northern Lights hadn't shone . . .*

He closed his eyes and tried to think. His senses weren't working. He opened his eyes and thought how beautiful the river looked.

He remembered something Father Topo had once told him.

Magic can be found everywhere, if you know how to look for it.

'Magic *is* here,' Father Christmas told himself.

And where there was magic, there was hope. He stared at the ripples on the river, moving again, like wrinkles on old skin, and he made a wish that someone would guide him to Amelia and then, right at that moment, above the wind, there was a sound.

The sound was: *miaow.*

A cat! Right beside him on the bench. A black cat. The very blackest cat he had ever seen. A cat that seemed to have been made from the night itself.

Except for a tiny bit of white fur on the end of its tail.

'Wait a minute,' Father Christmas said. He had seen him two Christmases ago, when he had been delivering presents. 'I know you.'

But time was moving and so was the cat.

Captain Soot was off, tail to the sky, trotting away from the river, and away from Saint Paul's.

Father Christmas followed.

48 Doughty Street

The black cat eventually stopped outside a rather smart door of a rather smart house on a rather grand street. The street was quiet except for a man and a woman. The man was wearing a top hat and had a twirly snow-specked moustache and the woman wore a long, shiny dress that almost touched the ground and was designed to look like her bottom stuck out a mile behind her. Or maybe her bottom did stick out a mile behind her. This was a very different part of London to Haberdashery Road. Everything looked expensive and calm, as if calm was something you needed money to pay for. The houses were tall and wide, and were set back a little bit away from the street, with doors that had to be reached by steps as if the house had fallen out with the pavement and had asked to have nothing more to do with it. The couple giggled at what Father Christmas was wearing. They had clearly drunk too much sherry at whichever Christmas party they had been to.

'He looks like that jolly red man who gave all those presents two years ago,' the woman said. 'Lionel, what was his name? Lord Christmas? Mr Pudding? Uncle Chimney? Father Jelly-belly?'

The man guffawed. A guffaw was a special kind of laugh that was very popular among very posh people in Victorian London. It sounded a little bit like an ordinary human laugh had been mixed up with a horse's neigh. 'Oh, Petronella, you are *such* a wheeze.'

Father Christmas liked to see people laughing. Even if they were laughing at him. 'Merry Christmas,' he said. And the couple both laughed a 'Merry Christmas' back, but time was slowing again so it was really more of a 'Me-r-r-y-C-h-r-i-s-t—m—a—s'.

Meanwhile, the cat was doing a very, very slow miaow, asking to be let in. The cat stared up at the smart black door and its Christmas wreath as Father Christmas took note of the address. 48 Doughty Street. He saw the house had three floors, and through the large window on the middle floor there was a man up late writing at a desk. The man noticed Father Christmas and the cat and then very, very slowly he disappeared from his desk. Father Christmas noticed the snow quicken up to normal speed and, sure enough, a moment later the man opened the door.

'Come in, Captain Soot,' he said to the cat and opened the door wide. The cat disappeared inside.

The man was quite short, for a human, but still at least double the size of an elf. He had a very small black beard on his chin and was dressed in a purple waistcoat and striped trousers. He was holding a pen. In a dark and gloomy city he was quite colourful. Like flower blossom in a puddle. He stared at Father Christmas with sharp eyes as Captain Soot rubbed his head against his leg.

'What greater gift than the love of a cat,' he told the stranger in the red clothes. He said it in a grand way, moving his hands, as if every word was incredibly important and he was talking on a stage.

Father Christmas smiled and nodded. He liked this man and his waistcoat. 'The love of a reindeer is pretty good too,' he said.

'Well, I know little of reindeer but I will take your word for it. Now, a Merry Christmas to you.'

Father Christmas decided to come straight out with it as the man started to close the door. 'I am looking for someone called Amelia Wishart. This cat belonged to her once.'

The door opened wide again. The man was intrigued.

'And who is making this enquiry? At one of the clock on Christmas morning?'

'Just a friend of the family.'

'And a friend of reindeer?'

'I try to be everyone's friend.'

'And what is your name? My name is Charles Dickens.'

'Oh yes,' said Father Christmas. 'I know who you are.'

'Of course you do.'

'I have given your books as presents.' Father Christmas realised this man could help him but no one was going to help him without trusting him and the road to trust was truth. He came closer to the doorstep so no one else could hear. 'I am Father Christmas.'

And Charles Dickens laughed nervously. 'I am a writer of fiction, but that doesn't mean I believe in it.'

Father Christmas tried really hard to remember the children who lived there. It took a moment but he knew it was still in his brain somewhere. 'Did . . . did Charley like his chocolate money? And did Kate like the pens I gave her? And did good little Walter like his toy soldiers?'

'How the dickens did you know that?' asked Mr Dickens.

'Because I am telling the truth. And I am sorry to bother you so late at night, and at

Christmas, but this is very important. You see, there is not enough magic in the air to stop time. And the later it gets the less likely it is I can deliver all the toys before morning. Also, without magic, it's too dangerous to fly my sleigh. Reindeer aren't birds. They just drop out of the sky if there isn't enough magic around. And it needs to be restored. And that means there needs to be more hope.

'One time before, when I needed extra hope, there was a child whose hope was so strong it got the magic moving. A girl. Amelia's magic helped me travel from Elfhelm. That's where the elves live.'

Charles Dickens was shaking his head in disbelief and laughing. 'Elves? Excuse my gigglemug but you are clearly as mad as a fruitcake. I know it is Christmas, but how much mulled wine have you had?'

But Father Christmas carried on explaining. 'You see, two years ago, everything went to plan. But *only just*. There was *only just* enough magic in the air. *Only just* enough hope. And so I started with the child with the most hope. The one who most believed in magic. She got me and my reindeer on my way. She kind of made it happen. There has never been a child so full of hope. It was a whole world's worth. But now that hope is gone.'

Charles Dickens was dabbing his eye with a handkerchief. 'That is really quite a sad tale, but I still don't believe it. All that stuff about stopping ti . . .'

Stopping time.

That is what he was going to say. But he didn't. Because, once again, time had stopped. So Father Christmas knew this was his chance to convince him. He quickly put his red hat with the white fluffy trim on Charles Dickens' head.

Then he took five big steps backwards and stood in the middle of the street and waited for time to start again.

Which it did.

Charles Dickens gasped at how Father Christmas was now in the middle of the street.

'Heavens. How on this beloved earth did you do that?'

Father Christmas then pointed to the hat that Mr Dickens still didn't realise he was wearing.

'A fine hat,' said Father Christmas.

Charles Dickens dropped his pen in surprise. He opened and closed his mouth like a fish. Then it finally dawned on him. 'Bless my soul!

What wondrous magic. You really *are* Father Christmas. This is most remarkable. Most remarkable indeed.' He held out his hand. 'It is exceedingly pleasant to meet someone who is almost as famous as me.'

'But, please,' whispered Father Christmas, shaking his hand, 'you mustn't tell anyone.'

'Of course not. Do come in.'

Father Christmas spent the next ten minutes with Charles Dickens in his parlour. It was quite dark in there, with just one candle flickering away, but it was a very nice room, and they had some mulled wine to drink. Which was still warm.

Father Christmas learned that Amelia had been sent to Creeper's Workhouse – 'the very worst workhouse in the whole of London'.

'I must save her.'

'What? This instant?'

'Absolutely,' said Father Christmas. 'It has to be tonight if there is a chance of saving Christmas. We can't have another missing Christmas. Two years in a row and there would be no hope left.' And then he realised time hadn't stopped at all for over ten minutes. 'I really have to go. There are only five hours until children will begin to wake.'

'But wait,' said Charles Dickens. 'You will need a plan. And a disguise. If the magic is failing you can't just skilamalink down a chimney and take her out of there. And also, what will you do with her? Where will you go? And what if she's not even there any more?'

These were a lot of questions. And they whizzed like fireflies around Father Christmas's brain.

'I think it is all quite impossible,' said Charles Dickens.

'There is no such thing,' said Father Christmas as Captain Soot jumped on his lap.

Charles Dickens laughed. 'Of course there is such a thing. Lots of things are impossible. Like writing a story when you don't have any ideas.' The laugh became a sigh. 'It's hopeless.'

Father Christmas winced. 'Hopeless and impossible. The two worst words.'

'I have been sitting upstairs at my desk every day for five weeks trying to think of a new story, but my mind is barren and empty. I've been getting the morbs. People liked my last story a lot and now I worry I will never be able to write another. Presently, my mind is as foggy as the River Thames in March. I have no idea what to write about next.'

Father Christmas smiled. 'Christmas! You should write about Christmas!'

'But it takes me months to write a book. How could I write about Christmas in, say, March?'

'Christmas isn't a *date*, Mr Dickens. It's a *feeling*.'

Father Christmas saw the writer's eyes light up like windows at night. 'A Christmas story? That's not such a bad idea!'

'See. There is no impossible.'

Charles Dickens sipped his wine. 'All right, well, I have an idea. You could pretend to be a night inspector. Workhouses, you see, get inspected. Normally when they aren't expecting to be inspected. Like at night. Or at Christmas. But you will need a disguise. I will help you. You can wear some of my clothes.'

So Father Christmas wore Charles Dickens' largest pair of black trousers. They were still so tight that when he tried them on the top button popped off and shot into Charles Dickens' eye.

Captain Soot laughed, but it was a cat laugh, so no one knew.

'I'll give you a belt, and my largest overcoat,' said Charles Dickens. 'And you will almost look like a normal person. Well, in a fashion.'

'Right. Thank you, Mr Dickens. I'd better be going. I have to find Amelia and deliver presents to 227,892,951 children before sunrise.'

'That's a high number,' said Charles Dickens. 'Almost as high as my book sales. Oh good luck, Father Christmas. I do hope you find Amelia. Please give her this if you do.' Charles Dickens handed over a signed copy of *Oliver Twist*. 'And do drop in next year as you do your rounds, won't you?'

'I certainly will.'

Then Father Christmas stared at the black cat with the white tip on its tail, gazing up at him from between Charles Dickens' slippers, and realised he had one more question to ask.

The Night Inspector

ather Christmas knocked on the scary wooden door of Creeper's Workhouse. It was large enough to be the door to a castle. Eventually, someone answered. It was Mr Hobble, the porter. Mr Hobble was hardly taller than an elf. He was a hunchback, but his arms were thick and his hands were big and strong.

He looked up at Father Christmas. It was quite a long way. 'What?'

There was a long silence. Father Christmas was expecting him to say more, but he didn't.

'My name is Mr . . .' Father Christmas suddenly realised he hadn't come up with a good name. 'Mr *Drimwick*. And I'm an inspector.'

Mr Hobble stared at Father Christmas's giant belly and his tight trousers.

'Inspector? You don't look like a policeman to me.'

'Why?' said Father Christmas. 'What do I look like?'

Mr Hobble thought. 'A giant puddin' with a human face.'

'Well, I am not a pudding. And nor am I a police inspector. I am a workhouse inspector. And I am here to inspect your workhouse.'

'Mr Creeper ain't said nothing 'bout no inspection.'

'That is because it is a surprise inspection.'

'Well, I'm sorry, Mr Drumstick . . .'

'Drimwick.'

'You ain't coming in.'

'Well, you are making a very big mistake,' he told Mr Hobble. 'When Mr Creeper has to close down his workhouse because I was denied an inspection, do you want him to blame you?'

Mr Hobble went pale. 'All right. You'd best come in then, Mr Dimwit. And you're in luck, because Mr Creeper is 'ere right now.'

Father Christmas then went paler than Mr Hobble. 'What? Mr Creeper is *here*? It's night. It's Christmas.'

'Exactly,' said Mr Hobble. 'See, two years ago, some malevolent being crept into the workhouse and sought to corrupt the children with toys and niceties. And Mr Creeper stays on guard to make sure he doesn't come back.'

Father Christmas gulped. 'Oh,' he said. 'Right. Good idea. Down with toys and nice things. Absolutely.'

So before Father Christmas could pretend to inspect the workhouse he had to go and see Mr Creeper. Creeper stood in front of Father Christmas, tapping the top of his cane with his long bony fingers. Father Christmas liked as many people as it was possible to like, but he found it hard to like Mr Creeper.

'So,' said Mr Creeper. And for a while he said nothing else. The word just hung in the air, as sour as his breath. 'Mr Drimwick . . . you are an inspector. Working for whom?'

Father Christmas thought for a moment. He noticed the bite-mark on Mr Creeper's hand. It was clearly a child who had done the biting, from the size of the pink scar. 'For the British Government. And . . . and the Queen.'

A smile crept onto Mr Creeper's face. 'I doubt that very much. You see, I have been running this workhouse for ten years. In other words, I have been running this workhouse since workhouses began. And I can safely assure you that you are not an inspector. Inspectors do not wear too-tight clothes and they don't smell of mulled wine. You are an imposter. Not an inspector. And so I have already sent Mr Hobble out to contact my friend Officer Pry at the police station, who will shortly be coming around to arrest you and lock you up for faking your identity.'

Father Christmas hadn't felt this nervous since he was a little boy. Magic had always

been his safety net. Here, in the human world, while the magic was broken, he realised there was nothing to protect him. 'I am not faking my identity!'

Mr Creeper came in close. His face was dry and grey. His nose was broken and twisted. His lips almost black. His breath as rank as a sewer. 'You are not a workhouse inspector and I believe very strongly that Mr Drimwick isn't your real name. You see, working here – with all the riff-raff of London – has made me smell a lie quite easily.'

Father Christmas wondered how Mr Creeper could smell anything with breath like that, but he didn't say that. He just had to stay quiet as Mr Creeper's nose twitched.

'Yes. No doubt about it. There is the scent of lying in this room. And if that is the case then you are committing a very serious crime, by pretending to work for the Queen. Very serious indeed. Punishable by death.' Father Christmas gulped. 'So unless you have a letter from Her Royal Highness Queen Victoria herself in your pocket, then you are in very big trouble indeed!'

A letter from Queen Victoria? Of course! That is exactly what he *did* have. So he put his hand in his pocket and handed it over. And Mr Creeper stared at the writing and the royal seal and he kept staring and staring and staring until eventually he forced a smile and his head tilted to the side and he held out one of his bony hands.

'Well, Mr Drimwick! It's an honour to meet you. I am sorry for that little misunderstanding. Now, when would you like to begin the inspection?'

'Right now,' said Father Christmas.

Mr Creeper's eyes widened. 'Right . . . *now?*'

'Yes.'

And Mr Creeper could do nothing but think of that letter from the Queen and nod his head and say, 'Well then, let's make a start, shall we?'

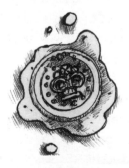

A Ghostly Place

The workhouse was a dark place, even in daylight, so at night it was like walking around a building made of shadows. There were a few oil lamps sticking out of walls in corridors and hallways but they gave off little light.

'As I am sure you know, Mr Drimwick, a workhouse is not a hotel,' Mr Creeper said as they walked through the empty corridors. 'It is designed to be as miserable as possible.'

'Why would you want to make a place miserable?'

'Life is hard, Mr Drimwick. Only a halfwit would want to fool people otherwise.'

Then Father Christmas heard something. Noise, from upstairs. Footsteps.

'Who is that?'

Mr Creeper smiled. 'Well, you see, two years ago we had another surprise visitor arrive unexpectedly in the middle of the night. And when Father Christmas somehow got into the building, we made sure we confiscated every single present he left. And tonight – just to be on the safe side – we have extra night workers. Not just the kitchen maid and people being punished on nightshifts but people on patrol.'

Father Christmas glowed red with rage and had to bite his tongue not to say anything. So instead he turned to Mr Creeper and said, 'May I take a walk around the rest of the place?'

'Of course.'

And Mister Creeper began to walk beside him so Father Christmas had to add, 'On my own, if you don't mind.'

Mr Creeper was about to object. His lip quivered like a dying worm. But then he remembered Mr Drimwick's royal seal of approval. 'Of course I don't mind. Inspect. Inspect away.'

Father Christmas walked around, uninterrupted. And he remembered it now, these corridors and dormitories, from his rather pointless visit there two years ago. He walked past a frail old lady mopping the floor and wondered what she was doing.

'Are you on the lookout for Father Christmas?' he asked her.

'No, sir, I have to make it so clean and shiny Mr Creeper can see his face in it. You see, I have to work nights now, since I did something wicked.'

'What was the wicked thing that you did?'

'I yawned when Mr Creeper was talking.'

He passed a boy, hanging upside down by his shoelaces which were tied to a pipe running along the ceiling.

'And what was your crime?' asked Father Christmas.

'One of my shoelaces was undone. So now I have to stay here till morning.'

He saw three more boys. Large teenage boys. They were standing by the fireplace, holding bricks and sharp knives and a red-hot poker. The fire was ablaze.

'Who goes there?' they asked when Father Christmas approached.

'My name is Mr Drimwick. I'm the night inspector. I have a letter from the Queen.' He showed them the letter from the Queen. 'So I need to ask, what are you doing here?'

'Mr Creeper has told us to stay up all night,' said the one with the poker, 'and if we see Father Christmas then we have to stop him and brand his backside with this.'

Father Christmas gulped, staring at the poker. 'Well, if I see him I'll give you boys a shout.'

Father Christmas knew the best chance of finding Amelia was to head to the dormitories. He remembered where they were. He had left the presents there two years ago. Presents that were confiscated before breakfast and which none of the children got to enjoy.

He reached the large empty dining hall, a particularly ghostly place. It was cold and draughty and had murky walls and high sinister windows giving glimpses of the night's dark clouds. A clanking noise came from the room to the side. So, on tiptoe, Father Christmas went to have a peep inside to see who was in there.

It was the kitchen, where large pans of grey goo rested on the worktops.

He saw a kitchen maid, illuminated by an oil lamp. She was wearing the inmates' uniform of brown sack-cloth. She was stirring something in a saucepan on the stove.

He slowly opened the kitchen door and stepped inside.

'Hello,' said Father Christmas.

The kitchen maid turned and gasped. She quickly grabbed one of the saucepans hanging nearby and threw it straight at Father Christmas. Luckily for Father Christmas he managed to move out of the saucepan's path. But then she threw another one and it hit him hard on the forehead and Father Christmas suddenly wondered why the kitchen was spinning. And then it went dark.

The next thing Father Christmas knew he was lying on his back staring up at a large piece of ham hanging from the ceiling.

Something Magic

The woman leant over him. She had rosy apple cheeks and her face was round, and made rounder by her hair being scraped back into a bun. There were sparkles in her eyes. Father Topo had once told him that you can always tell if someone is kind because kindness is the sparkle inside their eyes. But the sparkles in these eyes looked a bit more cross than kind.

'Who are you?' she asked. 'Sneaking in here uninvited in the middle of the night in your tight pantaloons?'

And there was something about the way she asked it that made him tell the truth, without even thinking. She may have just knocked him out with a flying saucepan, but she had a face you could trust.

So he just said it.

He said, 'I'm Father Christmas.'

The woman laughed. 'And I'm the Fairy Godmother!'

Father Christmas smiled. 'Ah. Hello, Fairy Godmother!'

The woman laughed even louder. It was nice to hear laughter in a place like this. 'You actually *believe* I'm the Fairy Godmother?'

'Why not? You said it.'

'Well, I'm not.'

Father Christmas laughed now. He had forgotten how peculiar humans were. 'Well, I *am* Father Christmas. But don't tell anyone.'

The woman was confused. 'Why would you tell me?'

'I don't know. But I'm serious.'

'Well, why are you spying on maids on their night shift rather than delivering presents?'

'It's a long story.'

The maid had never seen a face so easy to trust as the one she was now looking at. But still, Father Christmas! She'd heard Father Christmas was a man who had managed to fly around the world in a single night. How could this big fat man with a white beard do that?

'Do something magic,' she said. 'Guess my name.'

Father Christmas thought. He rubbed the emerging bruise on his forehead. 'The thing is

. . . the magic levels are low. That's why I'm here.'

'Excuses. Guess my name.'

'Jenny?'

'No.'

'Lizzie?'

'No.'

'Rose?'

'Nope.'

'Hattie? Mabel? Viola? Cedric?'

'No, no, no, no. And Cedric is a boy's name.'

'Oh yes. So it is. Sorry. I was just on a roll.'

She frowned. 'No. You don't seem that magical to me. I've seen more magic in a lump of coal. Now, if you'd please leave me alone I got to be gettin' back to work, sir. Mr Creeper'll be cross if I stand 'ere talkin' to you. Especially if you keep sayin' you are Father Christmas. He'll have both our guts for garters.'

'Well, Mr Creeper thinks my name is Mr Drimwick and that I am here to conduct a surprise night-time inspection authorised by the Queen, but I'm telling you the truth. And I am here to find a child. Without her, it might be impossible to save Christmas . . . You see, it's about hope. I need the girl who had the most hope two years ago.'

And then he looked at the maid's face and the sparkles of crossness were looking a bit more like sparkles of kindness, and maybe he had been away from humans too long but he felt just slightly in love with those eyes. A kind of warmth. It was a weird feeling, but a magical one, and he hadn't had a magical feeling in a while. Indeed, there was enough magic in the air that a name he had never known came to him, and he spoke it out loud.

'Mary Ethel Winters!'

She gasped. 'Never told anyone my middle name.'

'Born on the eighteenth of March, 1783. And you always sweeten the slop to make it more edible.'

She couldn't believe it. 'This is most peculiar!'

'And your favourite toy as a child was a little tea set. And your doll called Maisie, who you named after your grandmother.'

She was pale now. 'But how do you know all this?'

'Just a little drimwickery.'

'Drim*what*ery?'

'It's a type of magic, Mary. Based on hope.'

'You are a strange man,' said Mary. 'I could see that from the size of your trousers.'

Father Christmas looked at the large ham hanging from the ceiling.

'I thought everyone had to eat slop here.'

'That's Mr Creeper's ham. For 'im and Hobble and his policeman friend. No one else gets a look-in.'

Then a voice came from the doorway. Mr Creeper. 'Is everything all right, Mr Drimwick?'

'Yes, Mr Creeper. Just asking the kitchen maid a few questions.'

'From the *floor*?' Mr Creeper sounded suspicious.

Father Christmas could see Mary looking worried he would tell Mr Creeper the truth.

'I slipped,' said Father Christmas. 'The floor was so clean that I slipped right over.'

Then Mr Creeper stared over at the packet of sugar beside the stove. 'Mrs Winters, you haven't been putting sugar in the slop again, have you?'

Mary looked nervous. She, like everyone else, was petrified of Mr Creeper.

'I was just telling her I think a little bit of sugar in the slop shows great dedication,' said Father Christmas. 'And I am going to give the kitchen facilities full marks for that.'

And Mary smiled at Father Christmas with her eyes, which was the best kind of smile, and made him feel tingly inside.

The Girl Downstairs

F ather Christmas stood up. 'Now, if you don't mind, Mr Creeper, I would like to ask this kitchen maid some further questions about . . .' He looked around. He saw some butter out on a shelf. '. . . about butter.'

'Butter?'

'Yes. Butter must be stored in a very particular way.'

'I'll be waiting right outside,' said Mr Creeper impatiently. 'But can I ask how long this inspection will last?'

'It will be done before morning, don't worry.'

When Mr Creeper left the room Father Christmas was surprised to hear Mary whisper, 'Which child?'

He could see she believed him. His heart lifted with joy.

'A girl who sent me a letter. Her name's Amelia Wishart. She's ten years old, and I believe she's here in Creeper's Workhouse.'

Mary made a kind of whimpering sound. 'Oh, my heart breaks for that girl. The way she's treated.'

'I need to find her. You see, a lot is at stake. Her future. My future. The whole future of Christmas . . . Which dormitory is she in?'

'She's not.'

'*What?*'

'She's not in a dormitory. She tried to escape. He's locked her in the refractory cell.'

'What's that?'

'It's a room in the basement. Not even givin' her proper food. She has to scrub the floor. Scrub, scrub, scrub. Like Cinderella. I'll sneak her some food but it's risky. Mind you, so's us talkin' right now.'

'I'm going to help her escape. I might need your help.'

Mary nodded. She looked around the kitchen. 'I can turn this place into a trap. If you send . . .'

Her words died as Mr Creeper returned to the room.

'Now, Mr Drimwick, I'm sure you've seen enough of the kitchen. Shall we head out into the yard? Or would you like to see the dormitories?'

'No, Mr Creeper,' Father Christmas said slowly, 'I would like to go downstairs.'

'*Downstairs?*'

'I would like to see the basement. I would like to see the refractory cell.'

'No, I'm afraid that's not possible.'

'Oh,' said Father Christmas. 'The Queen won't like that. She won't like that *at all*. She could have you closed down for resisting inspection.'

Mr Creeper turned white at the mention of Her Majesty. 'The basement,' he said. 'Very well. Follow me.'

As they went out of the hall and down the stone staircase, Father Christmas asked if anyone was in the refractory cell.

'Yes, a girl. Been at the workhouse a year. But she came here as wild as anything. Really miserable she was. Asking for books to read. Moaning about the cold baths. Working slowly. Wanting animals to play with. Wailing about missing her mother. But we're fixing her.'

Father Christmas tried to hide his horror. 'Fixing her?'

Mr Creeper took Father Christmas through some windowless corridors.

And then they were there. A metal door

with a small square window. Complete with
bars. A prison cell. Creeper put the key in the
lock.

Unhappy Christmas

Amelia had been scrubbing the floor for three hours. Mr Creeper wanted the floor clean by morning. He was obsessed with clean floors, but even more obsessed with making her miserable. She stared at her own hands. The knuckles were sore from the soap. She knew there was no point in crying any more. The only aim she had now was to give up feeling anything at all. What was the point of having feelings if the only things there to be felt were bad?

'Merry Christmas,' she mumbled to herself. *What a joke!* There was nothing merry about Christmas. In fact, both this Christmas and the one before had been the most miserable times ever.

Well, this Christmas wasn't going to be miserable, because she was going to give up having feelings.

'I feel nothing,' she told herself, but then, to her horror, she saw a little fat tear fall from her eye and plop straight into the soapy bucket water.

She wiped her eyes with the back of her hand. And she tried to forget that magical morning two Christmases ago when she had awoken to see the full stocking at the end of her bed. No memories hurt more than happy ones that you can never get back.

In that moment, she hated Father Christmas as much as Mr Creeper. Father Christmas had let her know that magic was real, but what was the use of magic when it couldn't give you what you really wanted?

The sound of a key in a lock.

Then, that familiar voice, behind her.

'Stand up, Amelia,' said Mr Creeper.

Amelia was too tired and weak to do anything but obey it.

'Turn around.'

She turned around and saw that Mr Creeper was with someone. A man in too-tight trousers and a long coat with a white cloud of a beard. This odd man smiled at her. It was a warm smile, a totally different kind of smile to the one that Mr Creeper always had. But still, she could not smile back at the man. She wondered if she still actually knew *how* to smile.

'Hello,' the man said softly.

She said nothing.

And the man winced as Mr Creeper barked at her, 'TALK TO THE MAN, YOU RUDE GIRL!'

Amelia stared back at Mr Creeper with the kind of look that could have frozen water. But Mr Creeper wasn't water. He wasn't even blood. He was just skin and bone and hatred, and there was nothing a stare could do to him.

'It's all right,' said the other man.

'No, Mr Drimwick, it is not.'

'Hello,' said Amelia suddenly. She hated how her own voice sounded. The word 'hello' was a soft and trembling thing that died in the air. The man with the beard was looking at her with sad eyes. She liked this man and his silly trousers, but how could she trust him? What was he doing with Mr Creeper in the middle of the night? And not just any night. The night before Christmas.

'SIR!' shouted Mr Creeper. 'Hello, SIR!'

'Please.' Father Christmas couldn't help himself. 'Please don't speak to her like that. She's still a child.'

Mr Creeper's eyes narrowed as they studied the man. Amelia recognised the look on Mr

Creeper's face. It was called suspicion. 'Mr Drimwick, may I be so bold as to ask you your first name?'

The man hesitated, and in that moment had nothing to give but his real actual first name. 'Nikolas,' he said.

'Nikolas Drimwick. How interesting. My name is Jeremiah. Jeremiah Creeper. Now that we are on first-name terms I am going to be frank with you. A child needs to know manners and discipline . . .'

'And happiness. And laughter. And play. The three ingredients of life.'

'What kind of workhouse inspector are you?'

'One with a heart,' said Father Christmas. And he stared quite sternly at Mr Creeper. Amelia was now looking at Father Christmas. She was tired and she was hungry and soap water was itching her skin but her brain was now ticking. Tick, tick, tick.

Nikolas.

There was something about that name. Something familiar. Even though she searched her brain and realised she had never actually met a Nikolas. She had a weird feeling that she knew this man, but couldn't think where from.

'So, Mr Creeper, why is this girl in here and not in the dormitory?'

'Because she was caught trying to climb out of a window,' said Mr Creeper.

'Well, to be honest, I'm not surprised.'

'She wants to escape. So we locked her down here. And stopped her food. Except breadcrumbs and water.'

This man – this 'Nikolas Drimwick' – was turning red with anger, noticed Amelia.

'And you thought locking her in a cell in the basement was going to make her want to stay?' he said, the words flying out of his mouth.

'I don't care what she *wants*,' spat Mr Creeper. 'Who would care what a child *wants*? All that matters is what a child *deserves*. And I can tell you that I have known this girl for some time. Her mother was soft with her. She had it too easy. She was a rude and lowly chimney sweep, who was as grubby in manners as the chimneys she swept. I suppose if you are surrounded by soot all the time it dirties your soul.'

This made Amelia feel very cross indeed. She felt the crossness rising inside her like a brush in a chimney. She had *not* had an easy life. Yet there was Mr Creeper acting like she had been a young Queen Victoria or something.

And how dare he criticise her mother when her mother wasn't here to defend herself!

But then the tight-trousered Mr Drimwick said something rather peculiar while looking at Amelia straight in the eye.

'Oh, I don't know, Mr Creeper. I think you could still be surrounded by *soot* and be a *captain* of a person.'

Yes. There was no doubt about it. He was giving her a signal. He had emphasised those two words. 'Soot' and 'Captain'. He was telling her that he knew about Captain Soot.

And then something even stranger happened. He moved. The man *moved*. Not stepped or walked but moved *without anyone seeing*. He was now standing a step away from where he had been. And not just that. Something had happened in between. She had imagined he had leant into her ear and whispered, 'I am not Mr Drimwick. I am Father Christmas, and I am here to help you escape this place.'

She had imagined that he had called to his reindeer, Blitzen, at the top of his voice.

But how could that have happened in the fraction of a second?

'Mr Drimwick, you really are a very strange man,' said Mr Creeper, with dry amusement.

'Yes,' said Amelia, trying to give Father Christmas a clue that she knew what was going on. 'Like a captain. I understand.'

Amelia stared at Father Christmas and tried to send a message with nothing but her eyes. The message was: *You've got to get me out of here. It's horrible in here. I can't stand another day!*

And Father Christmas was quite good at understanding the language of eyes.

'Well, Mr Drimwick, I assume you have seen enough!' said Mr Creeper. 'Let's find somewhere else for you to inspect, shall we?'

Amelia felt a desperate sinking feeling in her stomach at the thought that she was going to be left in that basement cell. And she realised that something she thought had died was still inside her.

Hope.

The hope of escaping.

The hope of a better life.

The hope of finding Captain Soot.

The hope of being happy again.

Father Christmas seemed to understand all this too, because he winked at Amelia. It was a very small wink. Too small for Mr Creeper to spot. But it was there. And the wink seemed to say, 'It's time.'

Mr Creeper's Shoelaces

ather Christmas pointed at Mr Creeper's shoes and said, 'Look, your shoelaces have come undone.'

And Mr Creeper looked down and frowned. 'That is impossible. My shoelaces are always double-tied. They never come undone. And yet, you are right. They are undone . . . Amelia, tie my shoelace!'

Amelia hesitated for a second, then she crouched down and tied the shoelace. Just as Father Christmas was working out what to do, Amelia stood up quickly and pushed Mr Creeper hard, with all the force inside her, with every last piece of feeling she had, and he toppled back as Amelia ran out of the room.

'STOP HER!!!' screamed Mr Creeper. And then he shouted it again. With even more exclamation marks. 'STOP HER!!!!!!'

But Amelia was out in the corridor and heading up the stairs. Mr Creeper stood up and tried to run after her, but his shoelaces had been tied together and so he fell forwards and landed flat on his face, his keys flying and landing near Father Christmas's too-small shoes.

'That girl!' he shouted. 'I told you she was wild! STOP HER!!!'

'You just stay there, Mr Creeper. I'll get her.' Father Christmas bent down and picked up the keys.

'What are you doing?' wailed Mr Creeper.

But it was too late. Father Christmas was shutting the door and already turning the key.

'Mr Drimwick. Mr Drimwick, I demand you open this door at once. Do you hear me? Mr Drimwick!' spat Mr Creeper through the barred window he was now locked behind.

'I'm actually not Mr Drimwick. The name is Father Christmas. Pleased to meet you.' And then Mr Creeper screamed a wail of hatred. 'Aaaaaagh! Hobble! Mr Hobble! I'm down in the basement! Get me out of here!!!'

Child on the Loose!

melia kept running. Up the stairs. Through the corridors. She knew that Mr Creeper's staff were on night duty, patrolling the workhouse, so she threw glances in all directions. She hoped Father Christmas was on her side but he had let her down before. She just had to get out. She was running past the dormitories, knowing she had to keep moving.

Then, just as Amelia reached the dining hall, just outside the kitchen . . .

'Gotcha! You wild thing!' It was Mrs Sharpe, grabbing her arm hard. 'Escaping the refractory, are we? Mr Creeper! I've got a child on the loose. Mr Creeper!'

Amelia tried to wriggle free. But Mrs Sharpe had a strong grip and a loud voice. She was trying to wake up the whole workhouse.

'CHILD ON THE LOOSE! CHILD ON THE LOOSE! EVERYONE WAKE UP! I NEED SOME HELP HERE!'

Amelia felt the grip on her arm go soft. And

she looked behind to see Mrs Sharpe had turned into a saucepan. Mary the kitchen maid had tipped a massive pan full of slop over Mrs Sharpe. The pan turned out to be the perfect size to fit completely over her head, and to trap her shoulders inside too. Grey unwanted porridgey slop splattered and dribbled all over her. Amelia could now break free.

'Get me out of here!' shouted Mrs Sharpe. 'Get me out of this pan now!'

But no one could hear what she was saying because her voice was just a sloppy mumble. She kept banging into things as she tottered around and then she slipped over on a puddle of slop and fell to the floor with a clang.

'Thank you, Mary!' cried Amelia.

Mary shook her head. 'No time for thank-you's!'

Amelia heard footsteps and turned, ready to run, but saw it was Father Christmas.

'Hobble's letting Creeper out,' he said, breathless. 'We've got to be quick.'

Mary smiled. 'Had a feeling there might be trouble. Let's wait here for them, then lead them into the kitchen. I've made the preparations!'

The sound of Mrs Sharpe clattering around in the saucepan brought Hobble and Creeper

to the dining
hall, their footsteps
echoing like thunder.

Then, once they were in view, Mary, Father
Christmas and Amelia ran into the kitchen.

'Stand behind the door!' said Mary.

So that is what they all did. And it was
Amelia who noticed the floor looked very
shiny, even for a workhouse floor. She looked
at Mary as the footsteps got closer.

'Mr Creeper likes us to keep things clean
and shiny. So I made the floor the shiniest I
could using the butter Mr Creeper likes so
much,' Mary explained. And then something
funny happened. Something so funny that
Father Christmas laughed his loudest 'ho ho
ho' in a long while. Mr Creeper and Hobble
arrived in the room at the same time, but

instead of coming to a halt they slipped and glided and skated and slid right across the buttery floor, unable to control themselves.

'Aaaaaaaaaaaaagh!' said Mr Creeper.

'Aaaaaaaaaaaaagh!' said Mr Hobble.

When Mr Hobble tried to stand he fell back onto his bottom, while Mr Creeper used his cane to try and get back on his feet.

'Wait!' said Mary, laughing too. 'This is the best bit.' And with that she untied a string next to her and a handle began to spin. With a whistle the giant piece of pinky-brown ham that had been hanging from the ceiling whizzed through the air. It landed with a heavy thud on top of Mr Creeper, squishing his top hat flat and knocking him to the ground one last time. He and Mr Hobble were just a collection of arms and legs like a crumpled spider.

'Quick!' said Mary to the other two. 'You've got to get out of here!'

Amelia's Last Dash

There were other people in the dining hall now. Mrs Sharpe had removed the saucepan and, though still dripping in slop, was shouting, 'Stop that girl immediately!'

A gang of obedient workhouse inmates guarded the nearest door.

'There's no way out that way, gal,' shouted Mary to Amelia. 'You're a chimney sweep, ain'tcha? Maybe the fireplace is your best bet.'

But Father Christmas remembered the fire was lit and he thought of the boys guarding it. 'No, it's lit.'

Amelia kept running, twisting herself free of the various hands that were trying to hold her back.

Mr Creeper's voice was now booming and echoing around the dining hall. 'STOP THAT GIRL!!! Everyone! Stop her! STOP HER NOW!!! We've got to stop her, Hobble!'

'What are we going to do?' shouted Mary to Father Christmas.

Father Christmas was about to shout back when above the commotion he heard a very faint tapping sound. A soft clicking coming from the roof.

Only he, Father Christmas, could have known what that sound was, because it was a sound he had heard many, many times before.

It was the sound of reindeer hooves landing on a roof.

'My deers,' he said softly to himself.

Amelia wondered what Captain Soot would do in this situation. She believed that cats were cleverer than humans, at least at escaping things. And she decided that Captain Soot would have jumped up onto the tables, and so that is what she did. She jumped onto the nearest row of tables and ran the full length of it, jumping off the end.

'I can't see her, sir. There's so many people in 'ere now. And it's as dark as a chimney,' said Hobble.

But Mr Creeper could see almost as well in the dark as he could in the daylight.

'There!' he said. 'On the tables. Look! She's running. She's going to try and get out the far door. Someone guard it.'

'Don't worry, Mr Creeper. I locked it.'

And Mr Hobble held up a large iron key.

'Very good, Hobble. Very good indeed.'

Amelia reached the door. Discovered it was locked. Then she tried to push the door open, bashing her shoulder into it.

'Come on,' she said. 'Come on. Come on . . .'

Everyone in the hall wanted to stop her from escaping, especially now Mr Creeper was there. The only people on her side were Mary and Father Chri . . .

It was then she realised that Father Christmas was heading away in the opposite direction. She saw him at the other end of the large room, turning his back and walking away.

Typical.

He was letting her down again.

Of course he was. What else could she have expected?

She felt anger flood through her like red hot lava and she beat against the large door.

She bashed her fists against the door in frustration.

Bash, bash, bash.

But there was nothing Amelia could do. And Mr Creeper now had his bony, ham-scented hand on her shoulder. 'There is no way out,' he told her, his smile curling devilishly.

Bash, bash, bash, bash, bash, bash, bash, bash, bash, bash, bash.

She gave up.

Mr Creeper nodded, satisfied. 'You are going to be locked up for a very long time.'

Father Christmas's Escape

There was too much noise in the hall for Father Christmas to explain to Amelia what he was going to do. So seeing the whole workhouse was heading – no, *charging* – after Amelia, he decided the best way to help was to disappear through the corridor at the back of the hall, which ran alongside the men's yard to the bakehouse where the fire was still roaring and the boys were still guarding the chimney.

'What's going on?' the tall rattish-looking boy asked. The one with the poker.

Father Christmas was quick with a response. 'It's Father Christmas! He's in the hall. They're trying to stop him. Quick, lads, or Creeper will be mad as hell with you three . . .'

The boys looked at each other. Nodded. Went pale. Then disappeared into the hall.

Father Christmas chuckled, which popped another button off his trousers. But then he was faced with another problem. The fire was roaring. How could anyone climb the chimney without getting burned?

As Father Christmas looked at the flames he noticed a thin stream of glistening liquid falling down onto them. It kept going, slowly putting out the fire.

Father Christmas stared at the fizzing coals and the yellow downward stream and knew exactly what it was. *Reindeer wee.* And most likely Blitzen's, judging from the colour.

It was a wide fireplace and Father Christmas remembered it was a large chimney, so it wouldn't require too much magic for him to climb up it. He bent down and stood on those warm damp coals and did his best not to touch the moist sides of the chimney as he closed his eyes. He stopped thinking and started wishing and believing he was standing on the roof with his reindeer, and indeed, a second later, there he was. And there they were. Eight reindeer. And the gleaming red sleigh.

'Hello, my beauties,' he said, climbing into the sleigh. He looked at the Barometer of Hope and saw it was glimmering brighter. 'Now, quick, we've got work to do.'

Amelia, held by Mr Creeper, could see Mary running along the hall, between the rows of

tables, towards her. Towards Mr Hobble and
Mr Creeper. She was windmilling the saucepan
with her arm, swinging it round in ever faster
circles.

'Stop her, Hobble!' ordered Mr Creeper.

So Mr Hobble obediently stood in her way.

'Lady with a saucepan coming through!'
shouted Mary, and swung her saucepan arm

back, round and up in a perfect circle. The saucepan whacked Mr Hobble square in the face, and sent him flying backwards. She then stood in front of Mr Creeper.

'Put the saucepan down, Mrs Winters.'

'It's Miss. *Miss* Winters. Never found meself the right man.'

Mr Creeper nodded at a ratty-looking teenage boy who crept up behind Mary and tried to yank the saucepan from her hand.

'Can I just say I wish I'd never sugared any slop for you, young Peter . . .'

'You do realise you are committing a very serious crime, Miss Winters,' said Mr Creeper. 'Violence with a saucepan. On top of buttering the floor and attempted murder with a very large ham.'

'Well, you'd know all about crime, Mr Creeper,' said Mary as she pulled the saucepan out of Peter's grasp, causing him to tumble to the floor. 'This whole place is a crime. It's wrong to keep people locked up like this. I'm not working for you no more.'

'I save people from the streets.'

'You enjoy the power,' she said.

'You're a monster,' added Amelia, wriggling to try and free herself from his firm grasp.

'I enjoy the power to clean society of all its dirt, yes,' snarled Creeper. 'To keep order, and teach manners, and respect . . . And so now, Mary, you will be taken to the police station, and, Amelia, well, you are mine, by law. I own you. Like I own every child here. I will devote my life to making each day as miserable as it can possibly be.'

'Drop dead,' said Amelia. She had never hated anyone or anything more than she hated Mr Creeper in that moment and she lifted up her knee and stamped down hard on his foot with all her force.

'Aaagh!' He dug his nails into her arm and started to drag her away.

But then . . .

A noise came from the door. It definitely wasn't Amelia. She was being held by Mr Creeper and facing the wrong way. But Mr Creeper had heard it too.

'What the devil?'

Boom!

The noise came again.

And it was clear that whatever was banging on the door wasn't doing it from inside, but *outside*.

Reindeer to the Rescue

ho's there?' asked Mr Creeper. There was no response. So Mr Creeper pulled himself and Amelia closer to the door.

This was a mistake because just then something sharp and pointy broke through the wood and jabbed into the side of Mr Creeper's head hard enough for him to feel dizzy and fall to the floor, causing him to let go of Amelia and lose his cane.

'What *is* that?' wondered Mary.

'A tree,' said Mr Hobble. 'It's a moving tree.'

Mr Creeper was struggling to get up. 'It's not a tree, you idiot. They're antlers!'

Then the door burst open. Father Christmas was standing in the middle of the doorway, wearing his red coat and red hair, with his reindeer and sleigh behind him.

The whole room gasped at once. Mr Creeper pressed down on his cane and slowly got back on his feet.

'It's Father Christmas,' one of the children

whispered, and the whisper spread like a cold.

'Amelia!' shouted the man himself. 'It's time to believe in magic again.'

The Barometer of Hope glowed bright now and Amelia ran over to the sleigh. Father Christmas stepped back and looked at the clock in the sleigh. The time was the Middle of Night in elf time and three in the morning in human time.

Amelia, obviously, had a hundred questions, but there wasn't time for any of them. She knew that the sleigh in front of her was the answer to every doubt she'd ever had about magic, and she ran to it.

'STOP HER!' said Mr Creeper, stumbling after the girl.

'Press the button by the clock,' said Father Christmas as he ran into the hall to get Mary. 'Press it now!'

Amelia didn't know which button he meant and pressed the 'LET MAGIC TAKE FLIGHT' button. The sleigh began to rise and hover and wobble in the air as Mr Creeper used his cane to try and pull the sleigh back down.

'The other button!' shouted Father Christmas. 'The one that says STOP!'

There was chaos. The hall was crowding

around Father Christmas and – too late to duck – he saw a hot poker swinging towards his head. It suddenly stopped, freezing motionless in the air a millimetre in front of his nose. The whole hall had stopped, in fact.

Father Christmas ducked under the poker and wove through all the living statues in the hall until he reached Mary. She had been in

the middle of swinging her saucepan at Mr Hobble again when time stopped. Father Christmas picked her up.

That's right. Father Christmas picked that time-frozen rosy-cheeked old maid off the floor and carried her like a rolled-up carpet on his shoulder. Right out of the dining hall and plonked her in the back of his sleigh. The moment he placed Mary in the back of the sleigh she began moving again. First her feet, then her legs, wriggling like fish on a boat, and then the rest of her, including the arm holding the saucepan, which kept on swinging and hit Father Christmas on the head again.

Slowly she realised where she was. And who she had hit.

'Oh, my. I'm sorry. I'm making a habit of this,' she said. Then she looked around at the sleigh. 'Oh, I say, this is fancy.'

'Right,' said Father Christmas. 'Let's get out of here.'

The Return of Captain Soot

o you *believe?*' Father Christmas asked Amelia. And she could tell it was a very important question from the urgent look in his eyes.

'In what?' she wanted to know.

'In impossibility.'

And, right at that moment, outside the workhouse and outside time, floating in the air in a gleaming red sleigh, and seated next to Father Christmas, she knew there was only one real answer. 'Yes,' she said. And it was then that she noticed the small glass semisphere on the dashboard. She was momentarily mesmerised by the sight of the green and violet lights inside, like a tiny universe blooming into life as they glowed bigger and brighter when she said the words, 'I believe in impossibility.'

And a sudden urge came over her. A desire to see Captain Soot again. And just as she wished she saw a movement in the sack next to her. She heard the softest miaow.

'I visited Mr Dickens earlier,' Father Christmas told her, as she saw her furry best friend slink out of the infinity sack.

'Captain Soot!'

The cat's gold eyes gleamed when he saw Amelia, and he jumped up and put his front paws on her shoulder and licked her face as if it were cream.

'I thought I told you about licking faces!' She laughed, feeling the cat's warm purr motor against her chest. 'You're not a dog!'

She closed her eyes and kissed Captain Soot's furry head and inhaled the scent of his fur. All kinds of things really were possible in this world, she realised. And that was a nice feeling to have back. Maybe the best.

Mr Creeper's Fingers

Mary's eyes widened as the sleigh flew high up into the air, above the London skyline. 'Oh, my goodness, Mr Christmas. Where are we off to?' she asked.

'We are off to save Christmas.' And that was indeed the idea.

To keep time stopped and to deliver toys to every child in the world. Father Christmas drove the reindeer even higher into the air. Amelia and Captain Soot looked down to see the workhouse and the time-frozen people grow smaller and smaller below them. But then Amelia saw something that made her jump in shock.

Two bony long-fingered hands were clinging onto the sleigh. She leant over a bit more and saw the head of Mr Creeper. But as all of him except for his fingertips were outside the sleigh he was still frozen in time. She stared at him for a moment. This man who had given her the most miserable year of her life. His face looked angry, but also his eyes were wide with fear. (Mr Creeper, like all bullies, was deep down a very scared kind of person.) And, seeing that Mary and Father Christmas were deep in reindeer-related conversation, she thought she'd do something. So, she took his little clinging alive shifting fingertips and – one by one – pulled each one off and left him hanging in the air, about half a mile above the River Thames.

She looked behind and couldn't help but laugh, seeing him suspended in mid-air.

Father Christmas heard the laugh and gasped at the sight of Mr Creeper frozen in the air. 'Oh, my gosh.' He looked at Amelia and she shrugged smilingly and he saw her finger hover over the 'TIME TO START TIME' button.

'Oh, all right then.'

So Amelia pressed it and watched with joy as Mr Creeper fell down, screaming, and arms flailing, and landed with a splash in the Thames.

Captain Soot miaowed a few times over the side of the sleigh. 'That's for my great-grandfather Tom,' he miaowed, 'whose tail you used to stand on.'

Amelia had no idea what Captain Soot was saying but she stroked the cat and kissed his head and he licked her face with his rough tongue.

As they set off to deliver toys to every child in the world, Father Christmas introduced the reindeer.

'And that one on the left, second from the front, that's Comet, who has a little white streak on his forehead . . . And that one there, the dark one, that's Vixen, who is a mystery, even to me . . . and that's Prancer . . . who can be a bit of a handful . . . and that's Dasher, who keeps the speed up . . . and Cupid and Dancer, who are a little bit in love . . . and in front there's Donner, who is sensible, a safe pair of hands, and the best navigator . . . and Blitzen, who can be a bit rude with his toilet habits and is the strongest and, well . . . there has never been a better reindeer to have as a friend . . . Me and Blitzen go back a *long* way.'

'It must be nice for you 'avin' a friend up here in the cold,' said Mary.

'Well, I could do with some *human* company sometimes.'

And Mary's cheeks went a little rosy at that. 'Couldn't we all!'

'Right,' said Father Christmas, sitting back in the sleigh's comfy leather front seat, next to Mary. 'Are you ready for the *rest of the world*?'

'Oh yes,' said Mary. 'Especially Cornwall. Always wanted to go to Cornwall.'

'Ho ho ho! We'll be going a lot further than Cornwall.'

News from Father Vodol

ather Topo left the telephone, and the Toy Workshop, for five minutes to run over to the village hall. He needed to check the latest news of Noosh and Little Mim. Before he opened the short, thick wooden door, he could hear the hum of music and merriment. And inside it seemed like the whole of Elfhelm was spickle dancing to the festive sounds of the Sleigh Belles and inhaling the smells of cinnamon and gingerbread.

The song that was playing was an up tempo rendition of 'Your Love Smells Like Gingerbread (Yes It Does)' and so everyone was smiling and clapping and twisting. Well, not quite everyone. Humdrum was sitting down on a little red stool, looking forlorn.

'Did you check the whole of the Toy Workshop?' he asked Father Topo when he sat on the stool next to him. Father Topo looked at the long table behind them full of Christmas food. Gingerbread. Plum soup. Jam pastries.

Chocolate money. Cloudberry pie. He felt sad Little Mim wasn't there to enjoy it.

'Yes, I've had elves look absolutely everywhere. They've obviously gone off for a day out.'

'I just don't understand it. Little Mim was so excited about going to the Toy Workshop. And Noosh loves Christmas.' Father Topo looked at Humdrum's hands and saw they were shaking with worry.

'They're n-not at home,' quivered Humdrum. 'They're not at Reindeer Field. They're not shopping. They're not ice-skating. They're not here . . . Do you think we should phone Father Christmas?' Humdrum looked down and fiddled with the cuff of his tunic.

Father Topo knew this question would come. After all, Father Christmas had his sleigh and reindeer and would be able to do an aerial search. He also, these days, had more drimwickery in him than the whole of Elfhelm put together. But Father Topo also knew that the moment he told Father Christmas, the whole of Christmas would be in jeopardy again.

'I . . .'

Father Topo noticed the black beard of Father Vodol approaching through the crowd, like a storm cloud. He was walking straight towards them. His face couldn't have looked more urgent if he had had the word 'URGENT' written on his forehead.

'What is it, Father Vodol?'

'It's Noosh,' he said, looking worried. Which itself was worrying as Father Vodol hadn't looked worried for fifty-one years. 'She left me a note in my office. She's gone to the Troll Valley.'

Humdrum's jaw dropped open. 'W-w-hat? W-w-w-hy?'

Father Vodol shrugged. 'I think she wants to write a story on the trolls for Christmas. She's very ambitious. She wants Bottom's job, now that he's too scared to leave his house. I think your wife feels a bit above having to write about reindeer.'

Humdrum began to cry and shake even more.

'There, there,' said Father Vodol. 'If she really has gone to the Troll Valley there is only an eighty-eight per cent chance of her dying a really horrible death.'

'Oh no,' whimpered Humdrum. He said it twenty-seven more times. And then he said, 'Do you think Little Mim is with her? Oh, my goodness. This is a nightmare! What are we going to do?'

'Little Mim?' said Father Vodol, his eyes wide with worry. I don't know where he is.

As Father Topo tried to think above the sound of the Sleigh Belles launching into their new song about the new red-nosed reindeer who was being trained at the School of Sleighcraft, Father Vodol came up with an idea. 'Father Christmas,' he said. 'He's the only one who can save your family, Humdrum.'

'But what about Christmas?' asked Father Topo.

'Christmas!' said Father Vodol. 'Are you seriously saying Christmas is more important than the life of your great-great-great-great-great-granddaughter and her son?'

'No. Of course I'm not.'

'Good. Then you'd better phone his sleigh.' And then Mother Breer pulled Father Vodol onto the dance floor and Father Topo was left standing there, with Humdrum's expectant eyes upon him.

Amelia Gets Angry

melia stared out in wonder at the world, the wind whipping back her hair, as she stroked Captain Soot. She had no words, not because she wasn't thinking of anything, but because she was thinking of too much. Her mind was moving as fast as the air. A crazy swirling whirlwind of emotions – relief, happiness, sadness, gratitude, grief, fear, wonder, anger. The main emotion though, now, was a kind of homesickness. She obviously wasn't homesick for the workhouse. She wasn't even homesick for 99 Haberdashery Road. She knew someone else would be living there by now, and even if there wasn't, a house was just a house. No, she felt homesick not for a place but for a time. Maybe it wasn't homesickness at all. Maybe it was timesickness. She just missed those days when she was younger – seven, six, five, four years old – when she didn't know so much about the world. She missed, most of all, her mother.

Father Christmas pointed at the Barometer of Hope.

'You are part of the reason it glows so bright,' he told her as they flew over Prussia – roughly where Germany is on a map now. 'Because you believe in magic again. You see, you were the first ever child I visited. Because you were the one with the most hope inside you. You believed in every possibility. And that is very rare, even in a child. And now you believe again. You see, sometimes, a single child believing in magic – if they believe *enough* – is enough to restore order to the universe. Hope fuels drimwickery, and that's the main form of elf magic.'

'How did you become magic?' asked Amelia.

Father Christmas stared at her curious eyes, shining like tiny planets.

'I . . . I nearly died. I had given up hope. The elves needed to do a drimwick on me so that I came back to life. That's what gave me the magic. That is what made me see where the elves lived, because I suddenly believed in magic, just as you do now . . . I should have died on Big Mountain but I was given another chance.' The moment he said it, he knew it was a mistake, because two big fat tears had appeared in those eyes. He assumed she was sad.

But, actually, Amelia was angry. She felt the

anger rise inside her like lava in a volcano and she erupted: 'SO WHY COULDN'T YOU HAVE DRIMWICKED MY MOTHER? WHY COULDN'T YOU HAVE SAVED HER?! I DON'T CARE ABOUT PRESENTS! I ONLY WANTED THAT ONE THING! I HAD HOPED SO HARD! AND YOU NEVER DID IT!'

Mary tried to comfort Amelia. She put a hand on her shoulder. 'Listen, Amelia, it is terrible what 'appened to you – proper tragic. But it ain't Mr Christmas's fault.'

Amelia calmed down a little. She sort of knew Mary was right. But she couldn't stop this feeling inside her.

'I'm sorry, Amelia,' said Father Christmas. 'I got your letter, but when I was drimwicked I was on the other side of the mountain. I was beyond the Northern Lights. I wasn't in the human world any more . . . And besides, there was no way of flying to you last Christmas. There had been a troll attack and the magic levels were . . .'

'I'm sorry. It's just . . . I miss her,' Amelia said.

'Course you do,' said Mary, and she started to cry for the poor girl.

Amelia's head felt heavy with all these sad thoughts. So she rested it on Mary's shoulder. 'It's just strange, isn't it?' she said. 'You know, you love someone and they love you back and then they are no longer here. Where does that love go?'

Father Christmas thought about this. He thought about his own mother who had died after falling down a well. He thought about his father who had died years later, when he wasn't much older than Amelia. He turned to Amelia and said nothing at first. He felt so sorry for her. He wanted to explain that he had tried to come to her last Christmas, but hadn't been able to. He wanted to tell her that magic can't do everything we want it to, but it can make life a lot happier. But he thought it wasn't the time. So he said something else.

'The love of a person never disappears,' he said softly. 'Even if they might. We have memories, you see, Amelia. Love never dies. We love someone and they love us back and that love is stored and it protects us. It is bigger than life and it doesn't end with life. It stays inside us. *They* stay inside us. Inside our hearts.'

Amelia said nothing. She thought she might burst into tears if she spoke. So she was quiet for a while. And it helped. Then she noticed the Barometer of Hope.

'Why have the lights gone off?' Amelia said.

It was true. The Barometer of Hope was no longer glowing. It was down to a tiny little wisp of violet. And the clock was ticking forward again. Father Christmas stared at the dashboard and his rosy cheeks went as white as snow.

He picked up the phone.

'Hello, Father Topo. I don't understand it. We've saved Amelia, but the lights are still too dim.'

Father Topo sighed. It was the kind of sigh that says bad news is about to arrive. And it did. 'It's Noosh . . .'

The Troll Valley

Noosh had climbed down the craggy slopes of the Troll Valley under the moonlight.

She had carefully and quietly walked across the snow, stepping over goat skeletons and loose rocks, and gave a little shudder at the occasional giant four-toed footprint.

She had a plan.

It was a very simple one.

It was to talk to Urgula, the Supreme Troll Leader. She gulped at the thought. But, after that, she would be able to write the best story for the *Daily Snow* that there had ever been. And, as Father Vodol had reassured her, trolls never wanted to actually kill elves. But then she remembered the giant fist that had burst through her bedroom and grabbed Humdrum. Yes, it was true that Humdrum was still alive, but, thinking about it now, she was pretty sure that without the soap something very bad would have happened.

Urgula was the troll with the power over all the untertrolls and übertrolls. She was the leader because she was the largest. That's how trolls worked. The bigger you were, the more power you got, and the more roasted goats you got to eat. Noosh knew she lived in the cave in the largest mountain at the western edge of the valley. This was written about in *The Complete Trollpedia*, which Noosh had read forty-nine times while studying journalism.

Then, after a lot of walking, she saw a glowing orange light.

A campfire, in the middle of the valley. She would have to go around this if she was to get closer to Urgula's cave. Around the campfire there were trolls of every size. Untertrolls and übertrolls. Their large shadows could be seen moving on the snowy hills all around.

Noosh could see they were drinking large (larger than her) bottles of troll ale and eating roasted mountain goat. They were wearing roughly-stitched-together clothes made out of goatskin and they were being very loud, not because it was Christmas, but because they were always loud. They were singing the old troll classic 'Some Of My Best Friends Are Rocks'.

As trolls were on the slightly stupid side, it

was quite easy for Noosh to sneak up a bit closer and hide behind a hinglebush. She listened to what the trolls were saying, once the singing had stopped.

'Can you be 'memberin' last Christmas?' said one. The smallest. With one eye. An untertroll Noosh recognised from the troll attack.

'Yeah, Thud. When we be smashin' up Elfhelm! Why did we do that?'

'Cos Urgula told us to,' said Thud.

'Yeah. But why?'

'I dunno.'

'Why we be out 'ere?'

'We be waitin'.'

'For what?'

'Somethin'.'

Waiting, thought Noosh. And suddenly she had a very bad feeling. It was the kind of feeling that a mouse would have on approaching cheese only to realise the cheese was on a trap. *Who were they waiting for?*

Noosh gasped. She had made a terrible mistake in coming here. *What was I thinking?* She was very worried about how this conversation was going, as she cowered behind the bush, hearing these trolls, with voices as rough as the stony caves all around. And she was even more worried a second later, because that is when she heard another voice altogether. A small, high-pitched voice that she knew better than any other in the world.

'Mummy!'

It was Little Mim.

Inside the Troll's Fist

Noosh turned and saw Little Mim standing in the middle of the valley. He stood there in his bright tunic and had never seemed so small. His head was tilted to one side and his arms were stretched wide, as if expecting a hug.

'Mummy, I've been following you! I followed your footsteps all the way!'

Noosh wasted no time. She ran over to her son and scooped him up in her arms, but just as she was scooping *him* up someone else was scooping her up – scooping both of them up – and they were rising fast up through the air.

Three seconds later Noosh was staring at the largest face she had ever seen. It was an übertroll with hairy nostrils, warty skin and three eyes. The middle eye was in its forehead, but not quite the middle of the forehead. It was a bit too far to the left, as if the troll had been put together from a kit by a toddler.

'I'm sorry, Mummy,' whimpered Little Mim, from the darkness of the troll's fist.

Noosh stroked his hair. 'It's all my fault, shortbread. I shouldn't have come here. It's going to be okay.'

It's going to be okay?

Noosh admitted to herself that she had never heard anything so ridiculous. There they were, a hundred metres up in the air, being half-crushed by a troll's fist, and very possibly about to die.

But still, Noosh tried to stay positive as she waved at the troll.

'We mean no harm. My son and I were just taking a late-night Christmas stroll and we got lost and . . .'

The troll just kept staring. Her name was Samantha. She had a purple wart on her nose, shining like a Christmas bauble. And now there were other trolls behind her. Five of them. Six, if you count both heads of the two-headed one. One of them, the one with one eye, spoke.

'That be what we waitin' for,' he said. This was Thud.

Noosh decided to be honest. 'All right, listen, I'm a journalist . . . I work for the *Daily Snow*.

I'm their Reindeer Correspondent actually. And I was just doing an investigation. Well, not really an investigation . . . I was just planning . . . But the thing is, I'm not that happy being Reindeer Correspondent, so, you see, I thought I'd do this story about trolls that I was asked to cover. About what happened last Christmas. And the thing I have discovered is that it wasn't your fault. You are quite a peaceful species really. It's just that the Flying Story Pi . . .'

Just at that moment she saw one, fluttering above her. A four-winged Flying Story Pixie. This pixie fluttered down and whispered something in the troll's ear. Whatever it was, it wasn't good.

'You be here to kill us,' said Samantha. She squeezed them a bit tighter.

'No. That's not it at all!' shouted Noosh. 'Look at us. How could me and my son kill a troll? Think about it.'

'We do not be liking thinkin',' said Thud, scratching his head. 'It be hurtin' our brains.'

'Mummy! I'm scared!' whimpered Little Mim.

And Noosh tried to comfort her son, but found it was quite hard to do so, from inside the grip of a troll's tight, dry, goat-scented fist.

She desperately dug in her pockets for the

emergency bar of soap she had brought with her. There! She found it, but there wasn't much elbow room in Samantha's fist. Wriggling her arm she managed to pull out the soap, and she rubbed it hard against the troll's skin. It blistered and bubbled and started to steam.

'WAAAAAAGGGHHHAAAAAGGGGHU RRRRRRRRGGGGHHH!'

The noise of the anguished troll was terrifying. It was the loudest noise Noosh and Little Mim had ever heard, and it echoed through the valley like thunder. Samantha started to shake her fist in the air. Noosh and Little Mim screamed. Noosh in her panic clenched her own fist extra hard around the soap. The soap slipped fast out of her fingers and fell through the gap between two of the troll's fingers. She could just about see it fall and disappear with a small thud on the snowy ground far below.

'Oh, stinky mudfungle!' swore Noosh.

Just as the tiny bar of soap was flying through the air something else was too. It was hard to tell what it was because it was still dark, though the first grainy light of morning was beginning to appear.

Noosh saw it first. There were creatures,

pulling something. She would recognise the sight anywhere. It was Father Christmas and his sleigh.

Noosh held tightly onto Little Mim and they both peeped out of the cracks between the troll's fingers. They watched the sleigh hover in the air and saw that there were two people with Father Christmas. Humans. A woman and a girl. But that wasn't important. All that mattered was that Father Christmas was there.

'Mummy, we're going to be safe! Look! Father Christmas is here!' squealed Little Mim.

'Let's hope so,' said Noosh, cuddling her son.

Father Christmas slowed the sleigh in the air, around the trolls' heads.

'Let them go,' he pleaded. 'They are peaceful elves. They don't want to harm you. Let them go and let's talk.'

There were more trolls out in the valley now. They were hunched, crooked, knobbly grey-skinned creatures. One-eyed, two-eyed, or three-eyed. Sometimes two-headed. Some much smaller than others but all, in the emerging morning light, remarkably scary.

Out of a cave in the largest of the troll mountains, with footsteps that caused mini earthquakes, came Urgula and her husband Joe.

Urgula was so tall she blocked out the moon. Her hair was as wild as a tree in the wind. When she opened her mouth you could see all three of her teeth, each one the size and shape of a rotten grey door.

Another Flying Story Pixie was whispering in Urgula's ear.

Meanwhile, Father Christmas had landed his sleigh a good distance from the trolls.

'Listen at the front,' he told Blitzen and Donner. 'This is very important. Fly Mary and Amelia back to Elfhelm . . . Take the quiet route. Coming in from north-north-east.'

'What about you?' asked Mary, worry widening her eyes.

Father Christmas heaved himself out of the sleigh. 'Me? I'm going to make peace with the trolls.'

'Take me instead of them,' said Father Christmas as he walked over and stood in front of the gigantic Urgula. Her skin was as rough and pitted as the snowy rocks on either side of the valley. She did a burp. It smelled foul. Rotten goat meat.

'Look, why eat them?' asked Father Christmas. 'Elves are small and bony. Look at my big belly. You'd be far better off eating me.'

'Let the elves go, Samantha,' said Urgula, in a deep booming voice that sounded how a mountain would speak (if a mountain ever chose to speak). A Flying Story Pixie whispered in her ear.

And then, in that moment, Noosh and Little Mim found themselves being swung low in Samantha's hand before flying through the air. They held onto each other's hands and kept flying right out of the valley and over the Wooded Hills where the pixies lived. They landed on the soft snow of the slope not far above the Truth Pixie's cottage. They started to roll, faster and faster, down the hill until they were two big snowballs with faces sticking out of them.

'Mummy, I'm going to be sick,' said Little Mim, shivering. He was right. (We won't go into detail, but elf sick is actually quite a pretty purple colour.)

As the snow crumbled off them the door of the cottage opened and out popped the Truth Pixie herself.

'Hello again,' said Noosh breathlessly as she pushed herself out of the remains of the snowball. 'We really need your help . . . Father Christmas is in trouble.'

A Christmas Dinner

ather Christmas was lying down on a large raised stone in the centre of Urgula's cave while Urgula commanded the one-eyed Thud to keep him in place. Which he did by pressing his hand on Father Christmas's belly. It was as heavy as a rock.

Urgula's cave was vast. And the roof was very high. High enough for Urgula and Joe to stand up in and stare down at Father Christmas as another smaller untertroll (only three times taller than Father Christmas) sprinkled Father Christmas with herbs and rock salt.

'We be 'avin' a Christmas dinner,' said Urgula. 'We be 'avin' a Father Christmas dinner. You be small. But I bet you be tasty. Nice Christmas. Good Christmas. Thud, light the fire.'

'Listen, Urgula,' said Father Christmas. He tried to sit up but couldn't compete with Thud's strength. His magic wasn't working.

There was probably no magic left in the air now. This was just the simple laws of nature. And so there was nothing he could do about the massive heavy hand on top of him. He started to notice that the stone he was lying on was getting hotter. And as he saw the walls of the troll cave flicker with shadow and glow with a fiery kind of orange, he realised that this wasn't just a stone. It was a *stove*. Father Christmas was about to be cooked alive.

'What happened? I don't understand it. You signed the peace treaty. All trolls and elves were meant to live in peace. Everyone signed the peace treaty. Even the huldre-folk and the pixies and the Tomtegubbs and the Easter Bunny, and she lives a hundred miles away. What went wrong? Why did you attack Elfhelm last Christmas? And why do this today? It's *Christmas*. It's the time of peace and understanding and goodwill.' And then Father Christmas remembered the time when he was a boy, trapped in prison in Elfhelm. He had, in order to save his own life, killed an untertroll called Sebastian.

'Is this about Sebastian?'

But it wasn't about Sebastian. 'Nobody cares 'bout Sebastian,' said Sebastian's brother Horace, picking his nose somewhere behind Urgula. 'Sebastian were annoying.'

'Is this about hewlip? Because I'll have you know that, as leader of the Elf Council, I have made sure no one is allowed to grow hewlip any more . . .' (Hewlip was a dangerous plant that, when swallowed, could cause a troll's head to explode. In that moment, about to be cooked, Father Christmas wished he'd never had it banned.) 'So what is this about? What was last year's attack about?'

'We want trolls to be left alone,' said Joe sleepily, as if he was remembering a dream. 'We don't want elves comin' 'ere. And we definitely don't want your type comin' 'ere.'

'My type?'

'The 'uman type. And if you be goin' there into 'uman lands, they'll be comin' 'ere.'

'Humans aren't as bad as you think. And they don't know about trolls.' Father Christmas wondered what time it was, and thought of all those children who might soon have to wake up with no presents in their stockings again. *I have to get out of here*, he thought, as the heat started to singe his red suit.

'We don't like outsiders,' said Urgula.

It was then that Father Christmas noticed

hundreds of Flying Story Pixies darting around the cave, their wings glowing orange as they reflected the fire, wearing their shiny clothes, cupping their hands and whispering into all the trolls' ears.

'Don't trust 'im,' one whispered.

'He's a no good 'uman,' said another.

Father Christmas began to realise what was going on. 'What about pixies?' he asked. 'You welcome pixies here.'

'No, we don't,' said Urgula gruffly.

'But look! They are all around you!'

The trolls looked and they realised it was true. There really were Flying Story Pixies all around them. They had never really noticed them before, because the pixies were such delicate, whispery things who didn't want to be noticed.

'So they be,' observed Urgula, her mouth wide in wonder.

'They are whispering things into your ears . . . They are making you believe things that aren't true . . . They're hypnotising you.'

All the trolls looked a bit grumpy at this. One of the heads of the two-headed troll got so angry he said, 'Trolls be not stupid. You be sayin' that us big clever trolls be not 'avin' brains of our own?'

Father Christmas was getting really hot now. His back felt like it was burning as red as his coat. Even Thud, leaning over him, was hot. A bead of sweat dripped off his warty forehead and turned, mid-air, into a pebble that bounced off Father Christmas's stomach.

'I'm just trying to tell you what is actually happening. The Flying Story Pixies make you fear outsiders . . . You are being brainwashed. That's what's happening.'

'And what be 'appenin' now is we be going to be finishing you,' said Urgula. 'See, we was waitin' for you . . . We not be wantin' the elf and 'er boy.'

'But how did you know I'd come?' asked Father Christmas, his face as hot as a red coal.

This seemed to genuinely confuse Urgula. 'We just . . . did. Now. More fire. Let's heat 'im up.'

But then: a noise. A sound. Something cutting through the rasping of troll breath and the crackle of fire.

From somewhere else in the cave. Footsteps, maybe. Quite close. Urgula had heard it too.

'There be a noise.'

Thud heard it too, and dug his large grubby fingers into his eye socket to take his only eye out. It made a small plopping sound. He held the eye out at arm's length to see around the corner.

'It be a 'uman girl,' he said.

'Oh no, Amelia,' muttered Father Christmas. *Poor foolish girl.*

The Cracking Cave

Thud put his eye back in its socket as his other hand now roughly gripped Father Christmas's neck. The heat was unbearable now.

Moments later, a hairy untertroll appeared holding a wriggling Amelia. She was screaming very loudly. Thud turned to see what was going on and his grip loosened a little around Father Christmas's hot, sweating neck.

'Amelia!' gasped Father Christmas. 'What are you doing here?'

The hairy untertroll seemed delighted with the catch. 'We be got ourselves Christmas pudding to go with our lunch.'

'I wanted to save you, like you saved me,' said Amelia hurriedly. 'I owed you.'

'You didn't owe me anything.'

Amelia shook her head, which hurt her, as the untertroll was still gripping her hair. This untertroll was called Theodore and he had one large wonky brown tooth. But Amelia wasn't scared. She'd known so much fear in her life that she had finally run out of it. 'No. It wasn't your fault. I was cross anyway. Because sad things happen in life. They just do. But so do happy things. So do magical things. You did a good thing. You do amazing things. I was so happy that Christmas, opening those presents. So, so, so happy. Not because of the presents, but because of the magic that had brought them there. To know magic exists. You've made the world a better place. Whatever happens to us now, nothing was your fault. You're a good man, Father Christmas. You did a good thing.'

'This be boring,' said Joe, who like all trolls was allergic to soppiness. He picked his ear and looked at the wax. 'Let's be killin' 'em, Urgula. One each. Let's go.'

As Father Christmas thought about what Amelia had said he saw something outside. A kind of glow. As multi-coloured as the decorations on Prince Albert's Christmas tree. Green and pink and violet and blue. As he stared he felt a familiar warming inside him, like syrup being poured into him. It wasn't anything to do with the burning flames below him. It was the feeling of drimwickery and magic. Amelia had shown him how good and strong and how brave a human child could be. And that made him think of all those brilliant children who still needed to get their presents. It was the goodness of her that had helped filled the universe with hope. Goodness that had made her risk her life coming to save him. Goodness that created magic.

How much magic? He was about to find out.

He stared at the untertroll's warty left hand, the one holding onto Amelia's hair, and he wished for that hand never to harm Amelia, and suddenly the hand dropped the girl and the fist flung back, crashing hard into the roof of the cave. A crack appeared in the roof. Then other cracks too.

'What be you doin', Theodore?' asked Urgula crossly. And because she was cross she smashed one of *her* hands against the wall of the cave, which created even more cracks. (Trolls are famously bad at controlling their tempers.)

'Our cave be breakin',' said Joe.

'Yes, it be.'

'We've got to get out of here,' said Amelia, 'before the . . .'

But before she had reached the end of her sentence the roof of the cave began to crumble and a rock fell towards her head. Amelia jumped out of the way just in time, the sound of it crashing like thunder.

Then a voice. A voice that didn't belong to a troll or Amelia or Father Christmas, from somewhere else in the cave.

'Father Christmas? It's me.'

Oh no. It was Mary.

He could see her now. She was holding a stone and throwing it at Thud's head. It hit Thud hard, and green-grey troll blood started to leak out, sizzling into stone as it landed on the hot stove. He let go of Father Christmas's neck and stamped his feet, which caused even more cracks to appear in the cave.

As Father Christmas rolled off the scorching hot stove – 'Ow! Ow! Ow!' – he heard a large thudding noise. A falling rock had hit Mary on the head and she was now lying on the floor.

Father Christmas felt grief fall over him as hard as the rocks. 'Mary? Mary? Can you hear me? Mary?'

The trolls were trying to hold the roof of their cave up with their hands.

'You can save her,' Amelia said, feeling the hope rise up inside her. She knew her hope could help him. She knew now that this was how the whole universe could have so much magic inside it. By the simple act of hope. 'You can do it. You have to do it.'

Drimwickery

ather Christmas looked around the cave. There was no time.

No time.

No time.

And he saw in Amelia's face, even as the cave was collapsing, that hope had returned again. Light was leaking in through the cracks. The cave was now glowing a soft green that illuminated the whole of the inside. The trolls, the Flying Story Pixies, the rocky walls – everything was bathed in magical light. And the light was showing them the way out.

And it was there, glistening in Amelia's eyes too, that beautiful and magical green. The colour of hope. The colour of Christmas. It was clear to Father Christmas that it was her. She had brought the magic to him. Her and Mary. By coming to save him. And to help save Christmas. That was all that was needed for magic to happen again. It didn't take a sleigh or fancy clocks and buttons. All it needed was the simple act of thinking of others. And so he closed his eyes and he wished, harder than he had ever wished for anything. He wished for time to stop.

When he opened his eyes he saw Amelia, standing totally still. And not just her. Everything. Everything was still. There were stones and rocks hanging suspended in the air.

He had stopped time.

So, in that timeless moment, he got to his knees and looked at Mary, at her dying face, and he *hoped*. He saw the goodness in her eyes and he kissed her forehead and said, 'I love you, Mary,' and that was the first time he had said it, and saying it now he realised the truth of it. He loved her. They were outside time and so it didn't matter that they had only known each other for one night. He felt he knew all her past and all their future. He wanted to stay with her for ever. He could see their wedding day. The hope wasn't just an ordinary one. It had magic in it. Drimwickery. The drimwick, this unthinking hope spell, found goodness before it died and made it into life. And Mary's eyes flickered, just a little, like shadows behind a curtain.

'Mary? Mary?'

And then the eyes were fully open, shining up at him, and she was alive again.

'Mary,' he said, without even thinking, 'I love you.'

'I love you too,' she said, and she was speaking directly from all the truth and hope and love and magic inside her. And Father Christmas couldn't have asked for a better present than those words.

Then Mary saw all the rocks hanging in the air and her face filled with fear. 'Why is Amelia still as a statue?'

'We're outside time. We need to restart time to get her out of here . . . We need to follow the lights. They'll lead us out. You go. Go on ahead.'

Mary shook her head. 'I'm staying with you, Mister. I'm not waiting this long to find the love of my life and then leave him behind me in a troll cave!'

Father Christmas looked at the trolls. Most were busy trying to hold up the roof of the cave. But Thud was lying motionless on the floor where Mary had knocked him over, holding his one eye to get a better look at them.

Before he restarted time Father Christmas

climbed up on a piece of rock to take the eyeball out of Thud's hand. He placed it by his feet.

'Still gives him a sporting chance.'

So Father Christmas released his grip on time and shouted at Amelia, 'Quick! This way! Follow the lights!' He was about to leave but then had a guilty feeling filling his stomach. It was Christmas Day and he was leaving dozens of creatures to die under the snow. Now it was quite a strong feeling in his stomach, and he had quite a big stomach. It was Christmas, after all. Christmas. The time of goodwill to all. Even trolls. So he stopped and turned and told them, 'You won't survive. The mountain is going to collapse. You have to follow the lights. They are leading us out. Quick! Oh, and, Thud, your eyeball is by your feet!'

The trolls looked confused. They had been trying to kill Father Christmas and now he was helping to save them.

And so Father Christmas and Mary and Amelia ran as fast as they could, dodging the stones and rocks and moving through dust thicker than London smog until eventually they were outside in the open air of the valley. Just as the cave was collapsing trolls of all sizes

emerged from the rubble, crouching forward or on their hands and knees, coughing up dust. They stood there, all the trolls, like a small mountain range, in front of Father Christmas and the others.

'You be saving us,' said Urgula, between coughing whole clouds of dust into the night.

Joe nodded humbly by her side. 'Thank you. You be changin' my mind 'bout 'umans,' he said.

'Be we not still killin' 'em?' asked Thud.

'Kill 'im,' said the two-headed troll's right head (the wartier one).

'Leave 'im be!' said the two-headed troll's left head (the kinder, beardier one).

And while the two-headed troll had a fight with itself, Urgula thought. Then she said, 'I be confused. Cos you be good and kind, Father Christmas. I be knowin'. But it not be what we be told.'

'It is true,' came a voice.

Everyone turned around and looked to see a small wingless pixie standing with her arms folded and staring up at Urgula with truth in her eyes.

Footprints in the Snow

'Truth Pixie!' cheered Father Christmas. Amelia looked at this little creature in the moonlight. She also looked at the two slightly less small creatures with pointed ears, mother and child elves, on either side. The pixie was half the size of the elves, dressed in a yellow tunic, with a delicately mischievous little face. Amelia thought she was the cutest thing she had ever seen. But she also wondered if the trolls were about to kill them, and suddenly Creeper's Workhouse didn't seem quite so bad after all.

'The Truth Pixie is right. Father Christmas is the kindest man of all,' Amelia told the trolls.

The Truth Pixie, after a gentle nudge from Noosh, carried on saying what she had to say. 'It's true. Father Christmas *is* good. And he does a *very* good thing, trying to make the human world a little less miserable. That doesn't put any of us in any danger. Humans are too busy thinking of themselves to come and bother us. The Flying Story Pixies are telling you lies. I don't know why they are doing this, but every pixie I know is talking about it. They are making you look even more foolish than you already are. Which is pretty foolish, to be honest.'

'Liar!' said Thud, thumping his foot on the ground and shaking the valley, so that snow shook off the craggy hills and mountains all around.

'She no' be lying,' said Joe as he scratched his bottom matter-of-factly. 'She be a Truth Pixie.'

Urgula pointed a giant, sofa-sized warty finger at Amelia and Mary. 'But them be 'umans.'

Amelia took a deep breath and stepped forward in the snow. 'We were saved. Father Christmas saved us, because we were in trouble. That's why we're here. And he saved you too, and I really think you should try being a bit grateful, rather than being such big bullies.'

Little Mim clapped his hands at this. He liked Amelia already.

Urgula leant forward and breathed on Amelia. Amelia tried not to be sick, because troll breath was even worse than Mr Creeper's had been. Like cabbages mixed with goat poo and shoe sweat.

'You be brave, 'uman girl,' said Urgula.

'Thank you. Can we go now? It's just that Father Christmas has a lot of presents to give out.'

And just at that moment a Flying Story Pixie came and whispered something in Urgula's ear and Urgula bashed the pixie away. 'Be gone, pixies! Be in our ears no more!' And the pixie sped and tumbled through the air and disappeared in the dark somewhere above the Wooded Hills.

As this happened, Noosh stepped forward in the snow. She cleared her throat and looked up at Urgula, the largest troll in existence. Her grey face was a quarter of a mile above her. Noosh pulled out her notebook.

'Excuse me, Supreme Troll Leader, I am Noosh, I'm a journalist for the *Daily Snow* – it's a newspaper, like *The Ug on Sunday* – and I have a question.'

Urgula stared down at the elf, the way you might stare down at something stuck on your shoe. She didn't really care about newspapers. Even the troll newspaper, *The Ug on Sunday*, was something she'd only read once. (To be fair *The Ug on Sunday* was the same every week – a large stone tablet saying 'TROLLS BE BEST'.)

'What be your question?'

'My question be . . . I mean, my question *is*
. . . why didn't you attack the *Daily Snow*
building last year? Your trolls demolished the
whole of Elfhelm but they didn't touch the
Daily Snow.'

Urgula thought. This took quite a long time.
Her face looked in pain, and it probably was,
as thoughts give trolls very bad headaches.

'We be not attackin' *Daily Snow* because the
Word Master be a good man.'

'Who is the Word Master?' asked Noosh.

Urgula shook her head. 'The Word Master
at *The Daily Snow*. That's what they call him.'

'They? Who are *they*?' asked Noosh.

Noosh noticed that the Flying Story Pixies
were now flitting away from the trolls, and
heading back towards the Wooded Hills of
pixie territory. Urgula had noticed this too,

and she reached out and grabbed one of them. It was a boy pixie in silver clothes. Noosh had seen this pixie before. That very morning, in Vodol's office. The Flying Story Pixie had been at the window. Then she saw something in her mind. A memory from last Christmas Eve. Father Vodol's footprints in the snow, coming from the Wooded Hills and not the *Daily Snow*. Father Vodol had always hated Christmas. And he'd been jealous of Father Christmas ever since he'd taken over his role as leader of the Elf Council.

'Please don't hurt me,' the pixie squeaked at the troll one thousand times his size. It was like looking at someone holding the smallest piece of silver tinsel. 'Why you be whisperin' in our ears . . .? Tell truth before I be eatin' you.'

'For words. The Word Master wanted us to do it. And then he gave us good words. Long words. Words we didn't know.'

'I'm too tired for this but that sounds like the truth,' said the Truth Pixie, as she turned and began to walk home.

Noosh remembered the Flying Story Pixie she captured as a child and that long word they'd given it as an apology – 'miscellaneous'.

'The Word Master?' It all made sense to

Noosh now. 'Father Vodol. Father Vodol *loves* words.'

Father Christmas stared at Noosh. 'Did he send you here today?'

Noosh nodded. 'Yes.'

Urgula looked sad in the moonlight. A big fat troll tear fell from her cheek and the stone landed right next to Amelia. She let the pixie go. 'We be wrong. But we be sorry. We be punishin' the Word Master.'

Father Christmas shook his head. 'No, no. Don't you worry about the Word Master, I mean Father Vodol. The Elf Council will deal with him. All we ask is that you leave us in peace and don't go listening to any Flying Story Pixies in future. Now, we've got quite a lot of work to do before morning, so . . .'

Urgula nodded. Thud looked disappointed. Then Father Christmas and the others ran across the rocky landscape and back to the sleigh. Amelia got there first, and Captain Soot wriggled out of the infinity sack where he was hiding.

'I've just met some real-life trolls,' Amelia said to Captain Soot. 'And seen some pixies. And look, here are some elves. This is Noosh and this is . . .'

Noosh rubbed her son's hair as they sat in the back of the sleigh. 'He's called Little Mim.'

Captain Soot miaowed and stroked his head against Little Mim. He was nearly as tall as the little elf. Horse-sized, Amelia thought.

'You look rather strange,' miaowed Captain Soot to Little Mim. 'But I like you.'

'Hello,' said Little Mim, to Amelia now, smiling. 'How old are you?'

'How old do you think I am?' Amelia asked.

Little Mim looked Amelia up and down. She was very tall. 'Four hundred and eight?'

Amelia laughed. Mary laughed too. 'I'm not even going to ask him how old he thinks *I* am!'

Then Amelia told Noosh that she wanted to be a writer too, like Charles Dickens. And Noosh went a bit red and covered her son's large ears because 'Dickens' sounds quite rude if you are an elf.

Mary and Father Christmas sat in the front of the sleigh and the clock was on the dot of Last Chance Before Morning.

Blitzen and Donner were turning their heads towards Father Christmas, waiting for his word. 'Let's fly, my deers!'

And so they did.

Home

ather Christmas picked up the phone and spoke to Father Topo, who had been patiently waiting for news at the Toy Workshop headquarters. Amelia listened and smiled, still hardly able to believe that she was overhearing Father Christmas talking to an elf on something called a telephone, while also flying through night clouds on a sleigh. 'They're safe, Father Topo . . . Yes . . . Yes, really! Tell Humdrum right away . . . It was Father Vodol's doing, so we'll deal with him at tomorrow's Elf Council meeting, but right now we've got some work to do.'

And so it was that Father Christmas took Mary and Amelia and Noosh and Little Mim around the world delivering all the toys. The Barometer of Hope was glowing full force and so were the Northern Lights. Amelia had never known anything so magical as flying through that wonderful, hope-fuelled light show.

'This is . . .' And then she realised there was

no word to describe how amazing it was. The sight felt beyond words.

Father Christmas turned and smiled. 'This is what hope looks like. You help do this. You help make this happen. Just by believing in magical things.'

And so they travelled the world. North, South, East and West. The thing about the world, Amelia realised, is that it really was very big. And there were a lot of children. And a lot of cats sleeping on rooftops that Captain Soot was fascinated by. (The largest challenge of the night was keeping Captain Soot *inside* the sleigh.)

When she wasn't keeping Captain Soot out

of mischief Amelia would pull out presents from the infinity sack – each one perfectly wrapped up – and try to guess what they were, with Little Mim. *A ball. A spinning top. A cuddly toy. A book. Chocolate money. A globe. A satsuma.*

While Father Christmas was flying over Paris, Amelia, Noosh and Little Mim drifted off to sleep on the back seat, but if they'd been awake she would have seen Mary take Father Christmas's hand and squeeze it tight.

'You are a wonderful man,' she said. 'Don't you ever get lonely, away from other humans?'

'Sometimes, yes,' said Father Christmas as they flew over the shimmering Palace of Versailles. 'It will be nice to have some human company.'

'So is it all right if we stay with you, then? I mean, it will take some getting used to . . . All those elf creatures, with their pointy ears and big eyes,' she turned and looked at Noosh and Little Mim sleeping with his mouth wide open. 'So, I know this is a bit forward, but I think we'd like to stay with a human at first. If you *are* a human?'

Father Christmas's face grew red with merriment. 'I'm a human with added drimwickery. Just like you.'

'So can I do magic now?'

'You could do magic before, my dear. I felt magic the first time I looked at your twinkling eyes.'

Mary wasn't into romantic words. So she punched Father Christmas on the arm. 'You charmer!' she said, but then had to hold onto that arm because Father Christmas had nearly fallen out of the sleigh.

'Anyway,' said Father Christmas, 'of course you can stay. My house is the only one in Elfhelm that you'd be able to fit through the door of without a squeeze.'

'Charming!' giggled Mary as Blitzen and Donner dipped in the air, ready to lead the other reindeer and the sleigh towards every child's bedroom in Paris.

'Now,' said Father Christmas, after a few thousand more stops. 'Amelia, how do you fancy riding this sleigh? Seeing as you've saved Christmas twice now.'

'Well, it wasn't just me this year. I think Noosh and Mary played a part too.'

Noosh punched her hand into the air. 'The girls who saved Christmas!'

'Girls?' said Mary. 'I'm fifty-eight years old!'

So Amelia climbed into the front as Father Christmas explained the dashboard to her. The clock, the Barometer of Hope, the button that stopped time and the one that started it. Amelia saw that the time was now ten minutes past 'Very Close to Morning'. 'Elf time,' explained Father Christmas. 'They don't do numbers.' He handed her a copy of his own book, *Sleighcraft*. 'See, Amelia, Mr Dickens isn't the only writer, you know.'

Amelia was a natural, Father Christmas noted, as the reindeer responded well to every tug of the reins. All right, so she very nearly caused the sleigh to crash into Loch Ness in Scotland, but that was only because she was startled by the sight of a large monster poking its head and long neck up into the air.

'Once you know anything is possible, you see all kinds of things,' explained Father Christmas.

By the time they reached Finland in the small town of Kristiinankaupunki, Amelia could land carefully almost anywhere. She did so on top of a small roof with a tiny chimney. Father Christmas breathed in the cold air. He looked around.

'See those woods over there,' he said, pointing into the darkness towards dark trees touching the sky like a brush in a chimney.

'Yes,' said Amelia.

'A boy called Nikolas used to live there. In a tiny cottage with his woodcutter father. He had nothing but an old turnip-doll and a pet mouse for company. He was a skinny, raggedy little thing. And once, when his aunt came to look after him, he was made to sleep outside in the freezing cold. But in a way he had everything. Because he believed in magic. Really *believed* that anything was possible.'

'I'd have liked that boy,' said Amelia.

'Me too,' said Mary, squeezing Father Christmas's hand. And after delivering toys to the seventeen children of Kristiinankaupunki, Amelia flew the sleigh back north to Elfhelm. She had no idea how her life was going to be, or how a human child was going to fit in, but she imagined it was going to be a lot better than the workhouse. And as she landed to the sound of cheering elves back on Reindeer Field, a smile slowly crept onto her face and kept growing.

'Why isn't it freezing?' she asked.

Father Christmas shook his head. 'It's elf weather. It's only as cold as you want it to be.'

Father Christmas noticed that the Truth Pixie was there with her new boyfriend, the Lie

Pixie. A small male pixie wearing green, and with dark hair and dark eyes. He was handsome. He was probably the most handsome pixie in existence. The Truth Pixie's pet mouse Maarta popped out of her yellow pocket, but on seeing the black cat with a white tip on its tail quickly hid again.

Little Mim jumped up and down with excitement, knowing he was about to see his father. And he was. Humdrum was running through the crowds towards the sleigh needing to see Little Mim and Noosh for himself.

Noosh and Little Mim saw the bespectacled elf who they loved more than any other and both jumped out of the sleigh to hug him.

'I'm so sorry,' said Noosh.

'I'm sorry too, Papa,' said Little Mim.

'You're alive! That's all that matters!' Humdrum was so excited he hugged them and picked his wife and son off the ground but – not being the strongest of elves – he fell backwards into the snow, with Noosh and Little Mim on top of him.

'Ho ho ho!' chortled Father Christmas. 'Now go, and have a merry Christmas!'

'MERRY CHRISTMAS!' shouted Little Mim, who just liked saying those words.

Father Christmas could see Father Vodol lurking at the back of the crowd. He would deal with him at tomorrow's Elf Council meeting. Right now, it was Christmas Day, and he needed to show Mary and Amelia their new home. But just as he trod onto the snow, he heard a low rumble. The elves looked at each other fearfully.

'Oh no!' gasped Humdrum. 'It's the trolls!'

'No,' said Father Christmas, realising that this time it really *was* his stomach. 'I'm just a bit hungry.'

And elf laughter filled the air.

'Well, luckily, we have made a very big Christmas dinner!' said Coco, the chef.

'Ho ho ho!' said Father Christmas, stepping aside so the others could get off the sleigh.

'So here we are,' said Mary with a chuckle as she looked out at the small elf buildings lit by the pink sunrise. 'Our new home.'

'Home,' said Amelia, softly, to herself. It was ridiculous, the idea that she could make a home living here, alongside elves and Father Christmas. She remembered what her mother had once told her, about how life was like a chimney. You sometimes needed to struggle through the dark to reach the light. As she looked around at the small snow-covered buildings she thought she might finally have done it.

This was the light.

And so she gently took hold of Captain Soot and stepped out of the sleigh and into the magical possibility of her future.

Acknowledgements

I don't have elves or a workshop but I do have lots of people I need to thank, who helped make this book the thing it is.

I must say a MASSIVE THANK YOU in capital letters to the following very good people:

Chris Mould, obviously, for his marvellous and magical illustrations.

Francis Bickmore, my brilliant editor, for knowing which bits to take out and which bits we need more of and for letting me write the kind of books I want to write.

Clare Conville, my agent, for her wisdom and brilliance.

Rafi Romaya for all her design skills.

Jamie Byng, Jenny Todd, Jenny Fry, Neal Price, Jaz Lacey-Campbell, Vicki Rutherford, Andrea Joyce, Caroline Clarke, Lina Langlee, Alan Trotter, Jo Dingley, and the 'Production Elves' and all the team at Canongate for their massive support.

Carey Mulligan and Stephen Fry for lending their voice magic to the Christmas audiobooks.

Andrea Semple, the human I love and live with, for her sharp-eyes, her Ninja reading and editing skills, and for far, far too many things to mention here.

My children Pearl and Lucas, for being the reasons I write these books.

All my family and friends.

All the lovely readers who I have met or been in touch with over the years.

All the people who have supported my last Christmas book, such as Simon Mayo, Jeanette Winterson, Francesca Simon, Jenny Colgan, Frank Cottrell Boyce, Amanda Craig, Tom Fletcher, and Tony Bradman.

Oh, and of course, thanks to Father Christmas for being Father Christmas.

Thank you all!